'*Columba's Bones* is written with [...]
the distance between AD 825 an[...]
like a thin curtain – a curtain no[...] the one David
Greig's characters are tugging at, hoping to get a
glimpse of the mysteries'
Times Literary Supplement

'A surprisingly humorous take on a Viking massacre on the
island of Iona spans themes of love, death and faith while
unpacking the brutality of the mythologised Norsemen
with comedy and romance'
Scotland on Sunday

'One of the most interesting and adventurous British
dramatists of his generation'
Daily Telegraph

'This is a jewel of a book, sparkling like the seas around
the island. Each word vivifies the island, its natural life,
and the inner lives of its inhabitants . . . the physical and
spiritual merge on this Holy Island'
Historical Novel Society

'A well-researched, engaging fiction which contemplates
a fascinating culture clash between Nordic paganism
and Christianity'
The National

'Thrilling events in an authentic setting with visually
stunning scenes make Greig's debut work unlikely
to be his last'
Inverness Courier

A note on the author

David Greig's plays have been performed widely in Scotland and around the world. These include *Midsummer*, *The Events*, *Charlie and the Chocolate Factory*, *Local Hero* and *The Strange Undoing of Prudencia Hart*. He is currently the Artistic Director at Edinburgh's Lyceum Theatre. *Columba's Bones* is his first novel.

COLUMBA'S BONES

David Greig

This paperback edition published in 2024 by Polygon.
First published in hardback in Great Britain in 2023
by Polygon,an imprint of Birlinn Ltd.

Birlinn Ltd
West Newington House
10 Newington Road
Edinburgh
EH9 1QS

www.polygonbooks.co.uk

1

ISBN 978 1 84697 673 5
eBook ISBN 978 1 78885 596 9

Typeset by Initial Typesetting Services, Edinburgh

Printed and Bound by CPI Group (UK) Ltd,
Croydon, CR0 4YY

Iona

In very early times called I [ee], IO, HII, HIA or IOUA — possibly from the Norse Hiöe [ee-ë] meaning island of the den of the brown bear. Later named ICOLMKILL (G. I Chaluim cille — island of Calum's monastery). Columba is a Latinised version of Calaman (G. — dove.), but the saint's given name was Calum. IOUA became corrupted to IONA in the 18th century through a typographical error.

—from *The Scottish Islands*, Hamish Haswell-Smith

Chapter 1

I is three miles long, one mile wide and sits – a heart in the sea – just off the west coast of Scotland.

It is made of rock, sand, machair, bog, stone, sod and pasture. A low hill, a boar's back, rises in its breast. On the west side, winds and waves batter the rocks, on the east, tranquil, sheltered beaches. The north is mostly pasture and garden. The south is rough and wild.

The waters around *I* are full of fish. Gannets dive among the rocks. A fierce tide races through the pale blue sound, carrying terns and puffins along on the white wave tips.

Small birds sing in the oak grove, skylarks rise and fall in the meadows, and ospreys soar.

Taken together, if you catch it in one of those sudden moments when it's set in a bright shaft of sunlight, *I* is perfect: a miniature of the world.

★

It was like that when Grimur first saw it, pulling hard at his oar. The ship's sail was fat with breeze, and salt surf sprayed into his face. His thick neck throbbed. Wind filled his ears as they slid forward over the whale road like the coming of a dream.

Grimur lifted up his dripping blade and turned his head to the west; just then, the sun broke through mobbing clouds. Pale, low on the water, soft, it seemed to him curious: an imagined place, half in and half out of this world. Perhaps it wasn't there at all.

His next pull bit hard into a thick lump of water. He pulled with all the tired muscle his stupid old body could muster. As he pulled, he huffed out a breath-shout: *Ho!*

Then Buttercock, Bloodnose, Eyeballs, Gore Dog, Puffin Face, One Ear, Chin Slitter, Fuck-a-Whale, Lead Fist, Shorty, Fat Dog, Denmark, Horse Boy, Madhead and Ghost Axe – the men of Helgi Cleanshirt's boat – breathed in, filled their bones with life-lust, heaved and shouted together: *Ho! Ho! Ho! Ho!*

*

It was just after Prime, and Brother Finnian was in the vegetable garden when he saw the red sail. He knew immediately what it meant. He knew immediately what he had to do. Finnian ran to the tower and rang the church bell as hard and fast as he could: a panicky *clang-clang-clang-clang-clang*!

The monastery had never had the best of bells but, at least when it was first cast, this one had called the brothers to prayer with a respectable *boing*! Now, though, its iron was cracked through too many hard winters, and its peal sounded like the kennel man hitting a tin plate to call the dogs for butcher's slops.

Finnian's heart thumped with fear.

★

Helgi's wooden war-gull flew over the sandy shallows and landed on the beach with a groan. Bull shouts filled the cold morning air, followed by a clatter of iron and the thump of boots on wood.

Grimur picked up his shield and heaved himself over the gunwales: sea-drunk legs, stiff shoulders. The younger men were already running up the beach.

Let's do this quickly, Helgi said.

Two shares of silver to whoever guts the first Godfish! Denmark yelled.

Kill the fuckers! the men called back with a merry cheer.

The gang of hurt-causers set off along the coastal path at a heavy jog. Grimur struggled through soft beach sand. Soon he dropped behind the pack. He was already out of breath. He'd started too fast. There was no way he could keep up this pace. If he tried, he'd be on his knees by the time they reached the monastery gate, barely able to stand up, never mind climb the wall.

He wondered if he really needed his axe. Surely the Christians were unlikely to put up a fight? He had a stabbing knife. The axe seemed like extra weight. Still, it looked good and it scared people. He decided to keep it with him, just in case.

At least it was a nice day for it: light breeze, lambs playing in the fields. You didn't want to be splitting heads in the rain. Grimur's palms had only just healed from the shaft blisters he got during the slave chase in Thurso.

And no midges.

All things considered, this was a good day for a massacre.

★

The wooden walls of the monastery contained a whirl of panic and fear.

Farmhands pulled the big gates shut and barred them with logs and props. Others found scythes and mattocks to arm themselves. The housekeepers and laundresses ran from building to building, looking for children and places to hide.

In the middle of it all, on a low grassy mound in front of the church, Abbot Blathmac called to his flock: *Brothers! Come!*

Tall, thin, tonsured in the old way, and with his arms spread for gathering, Abbot Blathmac was an oak of faith growing from Columba's pulpit.

Brothers, be glad. This is the martyrdom for which we have prepared. Today we will leave the bitterness of life and step into the infinite bliss of God's eternal grace. Rejoice! Rejoice . . .

Brother Fergus, the hunchback, danced.

Brother Malcolm bunched his hands into fierce fists and wept.

Let your fear fall away, brothers! Do not flinch, but walk towards the killing blade singing! Welcome the knife to your neck, for tonight you dine with Christ!

Brother Colm screwed his eyes shut.

And, after all, what is there to fear? A brief moment of pain, the last rebellion of a weak and temporal body, before our immortal souls leave our failed flesh and we dissolve into a glorious union with the clear, blue endless sea of God's mercy. Brothers, be glad! Sing!

Brother Eoin fixed his gaze on the abbot, envious of the old man's faith.

Brother Eoin, I feel unwell, whispered a young monk, a thin lad with bright blue eyes who was standing towards the back of the crowd. White-haired Eoin put his hand on Brother Martin's shoulder. *Don't worry, son* – his face was fixed and grim – *your troubles will soon be over.*

Battle cries and yells drifted over the perimeter walls.

The young monk's face was pale and ashamed. *Brother Eoin, I feel sick . . . in my bowels.* The older man understood. No one wanted to meet his Lord soiled. *That's all right. Quickly, get yourself to the privy house.* He shooed the boy away. *You still have time.*

The monastery gates burst open in a hail of splinters and screaming iron.

Abbot Blathmac beckoned his flock to kneel.

Brother Martin rose to his feet and ran.

*

Grimur stood breathless on the mud pathway and leant on his axe. He'd thrown himself into smashing the gate with a hail of demonstratively heavy axe blows – showing off to the boys, really – and now his arms were sore.

A ploughman ran towards him brandishing a carpenter's hammer.

Grimur smashed him in the face with his shield boss. The ploughman's face broke into a mess of flesh and blood, and he fell backwards into a puddle. The clear water turned red around him like a halo. Grimur bent over the man and wiped his shield with the man's shirt.

Then he stabbed him in the heart.

Buttercock, Bloodnose and Fuck-a-Whale were going in and out of the village houses, killing men. Waves of screaming rose and broke, rose and broke. To his left, Grimur saw what looked like a smithy. There were still hot peats in the furnace just under the eaves. He wondered if it would be useful to set fire to some thatch.

To be truthful, the whole raid felt ridiculous. There wasn't anyone serious to fight. Some of the peasants were trying to defend themselves, but there was no glory in that. Helgi could just as easily have locked them in a barn while they stole the gold. Perhaps the women would fetch something as slaves, but they still hadn't sold the Thurso wives yet. Where were they supposed to keep new ones?

Grimur broke from his thoughts. A farm boy rode towards him at a gallop. Grimur stepped out of the way and, as the boy tried to turn his mount around, caught hold of the lad's leg and yanked him off the beast's back onto the ground. The boy's head smashed on a rock with a nauseating thump. Grimur stamped on his leg. Then he cut his throat. The boy looked about fourteen.

Grimur sighed.

He really needed a drink.

★

Lord, have mercy
Lord, have mercy
Lord, have mercy
Lord, have mercy

Seventy voices rose as one. Seventy unarmed monks, seventy white cassocks clean as consciences, seventy holy bald heads full of the glory of God, seventy spirit-filled hearts burning hot in the chilly spring air sang:

Lord, have mercy
Lord, have mercy
Lord, have mercy
Lord, have mercy

Amidst the screaming, the crying, the begging and the fury; amidst the blood and the mud and the sweat; amidst the swirling, horrible maelstrom of fear and pain and want and lust, seventy simple human hearts stood around a carved stone cross of Jesus and sang:

Lord, have mercy
Lord, have mercy
Lord, have mercy
Lord, have mercy

Grimur heard the singing as he headed towards the smithy.

Lord, have mercy
Lord, have mercy
Lord, have mercy
Lord, have mercy

It was, he thought, rather beautiful.

*

Grimur wondered if there was anything of value in the smithy. He wandered over. The furnace was still ablaze. The blacksmith had clearly been working this morning. Inside the hut he could see, in the darkness, a hearth, a cauldron and a woman, sitting on a low stool.

A woman.

Grimur took out his short sword and held it in front of him as he ducked under the eaves. Tentatively, he entered the room – and then his head exploded.

*

Lord, have mercy
Lord, have mercy
Lord, have mercy
Lord, have mercy

Helgi, Gore Dog, Puffin Face and Ghost Axe strode towards the monks, heavy axe shafts resting over their shoulders.

Helgi felt a bewildered contempt for these pathetic celibates and their odd god. As far as he was concerned, their passivity made them authors of their own fate. If anything, this ostentatious display of humility stirred his sadism. Did they think they were better than him? Did they think they were special? Very well, he would be specially cruel.

Father! Helgi called out to the abbot.

Blathmac turned to face him, smiling, arms open.

Helgi was an ox of a man, layered in armour, metal decorating his beard. The abbot was thin and wore only his cassock. Someone was in the wrong place.

What do you want, my son?

Columba's bones.

Those I cannot give you.

Helgi punched the abbot in the stomach. The old man crumpled to his knees. A group of brothers leapt up and tried to push Helgi away, but Blathmac raised himself up on one arm and waved them away.

His face was bright, ecstatic, his soul already half-merged with its maker.

Don't make this any harder for yourself, whispered Gore Dog to the old man. Gore Dog was a Sámi from the Far North. He'd been brought up with different gods. The others teased him sometimes because he refused to kill children. *Just give us the reliquary, Father Abbot, and he'll leave you in peace.*

Blathmac gathered his breath. *I do not have the bones, my son.*

Who has them then? Helgi spat.

I . . .

Helgi smacked the priest with the flat of his axe blade. The old man lurched sideways. Bright blood squirted over the tussocky brown grass.

I will kill one brother for every minute you waste.

The abbot replied weakly, *My son . . .* His mouth was full of splintered bone and blood, but Helgi could still make out the words *. . . though you come in fire and fury, I promise the Lord will forgive you . . . Kneel and repent . . . The Lord will take you to his breast and forgive . . .*

Helgi was bored now. He drew Freya from her decorated scabbard and swung her at the bowed neck of the nearest monk. This happened to be Brother Adam, a ginger-haired boy of about twenty who was a remarkable illustrator of dolphins. Helgi severed his head with a single blow. Adam's last sound was an in-breath of disbelief.

A moment of uncertainty shivered over them all.

Abbot Blathmac raised himself to his knees. The old monk's face was at peace. His body was full of a tingling warmth quite unlike anything he had ever felt before. He felt it rise from the earth, through his feet, thighs, crotch, belly, breast, arms . . . and radiate out through him into the world to heal it.

I forgive you, he said.

And at that moment the Holy Spirit passed through every one of the brothers, bringing each a shuddering gasp of joy.

Alleluia! cried Brother Malcolm.

Alleluia! cried Brother Eoin.

Alleluia!

Even Gore Dog felt it.

Suddenly, the air was full of something like the laughter that follows a really good joke. But instead of laughter, these were great, heaving body breaths of love.

Alleluia! the brothers shouted as one.

Alleluia! Alleluia!

★

There had been a time in Grimur's life when the world was all possibility, when his body grew stronger, his mind calmer, when every day he felt increasingly capable: with poetry, with politics, with the sea, with women.

This was not that time.

Now, Grimur knew that anything he would ever achieve had been achieved already. Each task he undertook, he felt less capable than last time, his body weaker, his thoughts more anxious. His hands shook from drink, and he woke every day feeling tired. He was bored of wit, tired of politics and no longer appeared to be of interest to women.

The only skill he had left, the only gift which had been enriched by drink, age and failure, was poetry. The sand of his mind beach was rich in words, the mead of Odin flowed in his breast. Grimur could forge tongue swords to cut open the skin of the world.

If anyone would listen.

Which no one did.

No, Grimur had achieved little, looked forward to less, and now he was going to die.

These were the thoughts that swam in Grimur's shattered consciousness as he lay on the smithy floor, in the moments after his head exploded. He opened his eyes and saw the smith standing over him, holding a spade at his throat. What a basic mistake. Of course the smith had been waiting for him behind the door. Now, he was going to stab the spade into Grimur's throat and kill him. Which Valkyrie came for spade-killed heroes and took them to her bed? he wondered. A homely one, surely. Carelessness, or Dumb Luck, or Old Age. Not one of the more glamorous Death Maidens, at any rate.

The smith lunged at his throat.

*

The stables were burning.

Bring me those ponies, Helgi ordered. The unearthly noise of the animals' distress was upsetting him. *Bring me four and let the rest go.*

Madhead and Denmark lumbered off to release the animals.

*

Grimur rolled sideways. The spade sparked off the stone floor. Grimur thanked Odin. The smith swore in fear. Grimur dived at the smith's legs, grabbed them and pushed him face-first into the open hearth. The big man's beard sizzled and a burning hair stink filled the air.

The woman, who had been hitherto silent, gasped. Grimur saw her standing in the corner now. Flat against the wall. He'd deal with her later. In the meantime, he scrambled to his feet, spotted his axe on the floor and picked her up just as the smith rose from the fire, moaning, fuelled with pain.

Grimur swung.

★

In general, Helgi Cleanshirt didn't kill. He liked order, not chaos. Killing, like kicking a small stone down a rocky slope, could create more trouble than you first anticipated. In battle, clearly, it happened. Battle was a reckless and instinctive form. One lost oneself in its flow, and the Death Maidens decided whom they wanted to take to bed that night. Killing was an effect of battle, but not the point of it.

Raiding was different. When raiding, it was important to impose a paralysing fear on your targets. Fear made them easier to control and encouraged obedience. It was a good idea, then, to kill randomly and often when you were on a raid, since it would speed up the whole procedure. The sooner you had the gold, the sooner the raid was done; the sooner you were back on your boat, the further the distance between you and whatever local chief might set off in pursuit.

The less well-armed the community, the more important it was to kill. Unarmed people in one location implied there were heavily armed people elsewhere. An unarmed woman or child implied a husband or father nearby. An undefended monastery implied a particularly mighty king under whose protection it sat. Once the raid was over, these husbands, fathers and kings would invariably seek revenge. Revengers were a pain in the arse. So, to reduce their possibility, it was best to leave no survivors. No one to identify you. No one with clues as to your vulnerabilities. No one to whip up feelings of anger or injustice in kin or kings.

It was also helpful, Helgi felt, if the killing was done in a spectacular way. The more horror and dread the post-raid scene inspired in those who eventually discovered it, the less likely they would be to seek a fight with you later.

So, if everything went to plan, you could perpetrate one absolutely maniacal raid on an unarmed community, the kind of killing people would whisper about in horror, and thus obviate the need for any more raids thereafter. If every village feared your sail, the next time you came south on a raiding trip, you wouldn't need to raise a sweat. Locals, kings, fathers, husbands – they would meet you on the shore, arms heavy with tribute.

That's why Helgi killed small children by tossing them up in the air and catching them on the end of his sword. Some of his men felt that was going a bit far, but Helgi knew what he was doing.

Helgi didn't kill people often, and, in general, did not use excessive cruelty when so doing. But just because he didn't do it often, didn't mean he didn't enjoy it when he got the chance.

And this was a chance.

*

Even as he turned his shoulders, Grimur knew it was a good swing.

Sometimes you just know.

The smith lunged, and the axe fell, thunking into the man's torso with a sound like a knife going through an apple, and the smith's left arm fell off onto the stone floor.

There it lay, palm upwards, as if asking for something.

The smith looked at it, in horror. If he had had one moment more, he might have realised some of the immediate implications for his career. Shoeing horses was going to be much harder. Would he be able to operate the bellows? How on earth would he lift the anvil?

But the smith did not have a moment more. Time moved too quickly for him. After all, he was a smith and Grimur, however lazy, was a warrior. In battle, time moves more slowly for warriors than ordinary men. This was a well-known fact. So, in what can't have been more than a few seconds for the smith, but felt like five minutes for Grimur, the Viking had put down his axe, picked up his sword and stabbed it through the smith's chest, lungs and ribs until its bloody tip peeped out the man's tunic like a salmon's head breaching.

Grimur's eyes met the smith's in an awkward moment of intimacy.

Then the candle was extinguished.

Grimur let his body fall.

*

Helgi harnessed four ponies in front of the church, but where normally one would have attached the plough, Helgi tied the abbot's wrists and ankles. So that, if you had seen the scene from God's point of view, you would have observed Blathmac on his back, spread-eagled, with a rope and a pony pulling at each limb, making a Saint Andrew's cross of him on the paved churchyard.

Where are the bones?

I forgive you.

PULL!

So, this was how he was to die. He could hear the monks praying loudly, as much to keep their own spirits up as to comfort him during his torture.

But they needn't have bothered, for the Father Abbot was in a condition of replete peace. His courage had held. He'd always wondered if it would. Now he knew. He felt proud, almost smug. His ordeal would soon be over and, so far, it had been nowhere near as bad as he had expected.

At least it was interesting.

He was in agony, of course, but he didn't feel it as pain. He felt it as a kind of heat. In the same way that when you walk into the freezing sea, you feel burning. Pain, yes, but also *life*.

The whipped ponies began to stretch his body.

Where are the bones?

I forgive you.

Helgi turned to the field of kneeling monks in frustration. *One of you knows! Don't any of you want to save him? Don't any of you want to stop this horror?*

The brothers stared back at him, impassive.

The whole point of this trip was the bones. He had money and silver and slaves from the Church, which was fine, but he wanted a reliquary. A fancy silver reliquary of a Christian holy saint. Now that was a prize.

And now this feeble-minded old prick was stopping him from getting what he wanted.

PULL!

PULL!

Buttercock shouted from the back of the crowd. One of the monks had spoken. *He buried it, Helgi. This one said he buried it at night so none of the brothers would know where. Only he knows. That's why they're silent.*

Helgi looked at the abbot.

The ponies shuffled and stamped. A warm breeze, a moment of peace – this was Blathmac's chance to speak.

The sea was softly choppy. Gannets daggered the blue. Seals took the sun on the black scatters of rocks that fringed the green.

On the south of the island, children hid in the bog, skylarks rose and fell, newly born lambs bleated to their mothers, curlews whistled and peeped.

I sang out its being to the wind.

How could you leave this world, willingly?

How could you stay?

It is true, my son.

PULL!

Gore Dog, Ghost Axe, Denmark and Madhead each whipped on their ponies.

The brothers wept and sang.

After five, or maybe eight, minutes, it was over.

★

The smith's woman had moved behind the cauldron. Now, she was holding on to it as if she were concerned about it being knocked over. She had a little paring knife tucked in her underwear. If he lunged, it wouldn't save her, but it would hurt him. With luck, and if she were quick, she might get his balls.

Grimur moved slowly towards her with his sword in front of him.

She was a handsome woman, her hair light grey and cut short, and she smelt of honey.

He noticed she was hiding something behind her back. A hammer? A knife?

He paused.

She narrowed her eyes.

As Grimur got closer, he saw what was inside the cauldron. In fact, it would be more accurate to say he *smelt* what was inside the cauldron, because it was the scent which hit him first: a familiar aroma, as happy and enfolding to Grimur as a milky breast to a hungry baby.

Mead.

A great metal vat full of golden, sunset-coloured, sweetly herbed mead.

Grimur inhaled. He drew the intoxicating mist deeply into his chest. Still holding his sword, he dipped a finger into the liquid and brought it up to his mouth. A choir of flavours sang on his tongue: first, in sudden chords, peat smoke, honey, raspberry, rosehip, armpit, sea; then, then in single voices, dill, dung, juniper, kelp.

It was extraordinary.

Did you make this?

She nodded.

Ordinarily, Grimur would have lunged forward at this point, either to kill her or subdue her for capture. She was fit and handsome, maybe a bit old, but if she'd made this brew, she'd make a decent slave. But Grimur didn't want to lunge. Grimur was tired, and curious, and, at heart, he just wanted to sit down and have a nice drink.

His eyes must have shown a moment's hesitation because just at that second the mead wife revealed what she'd been hiding behind her back.

A ladle.

Grimur laughed. He couldn't help it. A ladle?

She thrust it towards him like a sword. That made him laugh again. Then she waved it around, as if cutting and stabbing an enemy.

By now, tears were running down his stupid Viking cheeks.

She enjoyed controlling him.

His laughter was snottery and giggly. It wasn't the laughter of a rapist. It was the laughter of a boy. It made the mead wife laugh as well.

He put the sword down on the floor, then he unhooked his drinking horn from his belt and held it out to her.

She dipped the ladle into the sweet honey liquid.

They kept their eyes on each other as she carefully poured the brew into his horn.

Grimur put the horn to his lips and drank.

*

After they had beheaded the last monk, Helgi noticed the sun was low behind the hill. He became anxious about time. The smoke from the burnings would have been seen from Mull. It wouldn't take long for word to travel to the chiefs and villages.

It's time to go, Helgi ordered.

Madhead and Denmark yoked ponies to a farm cart. Gore Dog and the others threw the treasure they'd found into the back. Candlesticks, coin chests, silver goblets, decorative metal filigrees, crosses and robes.

Fuck-a-Whale and Chin Slitter roped the survivors in a slave chain. Another cart carried meat and grain. The sea-raiders then formed a convoy and carted their winnings down to the sandy bay.

Helgi supervised the loading while they waited for the tide to lift the boat.

They were just securing the load on the deck when Ghost Axe and Buttercock came back from the village carrying an armoured warrior's body.

Hey, hey! called Helgi. *Is that one of ours?*

Yes, said Buttercock.

Who is it?

He hadn't noticed anyone missing.

Grimur, Ghost Axe said sadly.

Helgi looked at the limp, bearded figure held between the two warriors like a sack.

Who?

*

After they'd dug a quick grave – Helgi was becoming increasingly concerned about time – the men carefully placed Grimur in it. Face up. Smiling.

Buttercock laid his meat knife into the corpse's hand. He'd need it to feast with the heroes in Valhalla tonight.

What shall we do with his sword? he asked.

Give it to Horse Boy, Helgi said.

But the dead guy might need it.

No, he won't. He's already walking in the dark woods of death. Soon he'll see the light and the doors of Valhalla. He'll knock, and the door slaves will recognise him. Welcome, Gunnar, they'll say.

It's Grimur, said Ghost Axe.

Welcome, Grimur, Helgi continued. *And then Odin will*

welcome him to the heaving mead benches. 'Shift your arses, you heroes. Make room for Grimur ...' He looked down at the bearded, smiling, fat man in the grave. *What was his nickname?*

No one knew. Some shouted out suggestions.

Pudger?

Old Guy?

I don't think he had a nickname, Helgi. He's only been with us for a year or so.

Oh, that's a shame. Even Helgi seemed moved by the brutal transience of our presence in life at that moment. *Nevertheless, he will sit and Odin will say, 'Welcome, Grimur. No-Name. You died the death of a ...'* How did he die?

We found him on the floor of the smithy.

Was he wounded?

No.

So, did he die in battle?

I think he just collapsed.

Helgi considered. *Nevertheless, he was a good guy.*

The others agreed.

He was solid.

Always there.

Not bad with an axe.

Are we sure he's going to Valhalla, though? This was Puffin Face. He had a nasal voice. It was hard to listen to. *Are we suuure?*

Truthfully, nobody really liked him.

Sure — why not? said Helgi.

It's not technically a death in battle?

He died during a battle, offered Buttercock.

He collapsed.

From the effort of fighting. Ghost Axe felt he needed to defend his comrade, even if he couldn't really recall why.

He died a Viking. Helgi settled it. *Put his axe in the ground.*

What else shall we put in? asked Buttercock. *Who's got a gruel bowl? Does anyone have a gruel bowl they can spare? Or a bag of oats?*

The men shook their heads.

That's enough, said Helgi. *Buttercock, put his shield over him and fill in the grave. The rest of you finish loading the chests. Tie down the women. Prepare to launch.*

Buttercock laid the bloodstained shield over the dead man's chest and chin. *Travel well, No-Name.*

He filled in the grave with earth and turf, laid a stone on top of it, then jogged back down the hill and waded out to the boat.

Ho! cried Gore Dog.

Ho! the men replied.

Oars bit the cold water.

The setting sun turned copper.

Helgi's red sail disappeared over the northern horizon.

Chapter 2

Martin was up to his knees in a sea of shit when he heard movement above. He'd long ago retched up every last ounce of his insides and was delirious with sleeplessness and shame.

First, he heard footsteps, then a stream of warm piss fell on his head.

Martin held his breath and prayed.

Holy God, Holy Mighty, Holy Immortal, I know that I am nothing and You are boundless beyond reckoning. I know that I am a sparrow flying through an oak grove while You are always and everywhere and eternal. I know I am a coward standing in a pit of shit and You are creator of the universe, but, Lord, Lord, please, please, please . . .

The figure above him groaned and sighed.

. . . please let me live just a little longer . . .

A creak of the wooden bench.

. . . and, Lord, if You spare me, Your basest servant, I promise I will honour and serve the rule of Saint Colm for all the remaining days of my life.

He heard a dull plop beside him.

Your obedient slave, Martin.

He opened his eyes. The crap had missed his body. Perhaps it was a sign.

Ten feet above him, a man rose, pulled up his breeks, threw a cloth into the pit and shouted, *Domhnall! Domhnall! There's more bodies over here by the latrine.*

Gaelic! Alleluia!

The Vikings were gone, the king's men had arrived – Martin knew he was saved.

Just at that moment a gap in the clouds aligned so precisely with the circular hole in the latrine boards that a ray of spring sunshine flooded the privy pit in a honeyed flush of light.

Filled with gratitude, Martin sang Matins:

O God, come to my assistance!
O Lord, make haste to help me
O Lord, Thou wilt open my lips, and my mouth shall
    declare
Thy praise!

*

Domhnall of Crinan looked at the horrible scene and crossed himself.

Smoke hung over the monastery ruins, mixed with a thick grey haar. Wet burnt-wood smell and high death odour hung in the air. Crows and gulls were feeding on corpses, dogs burying themselves greedily in the bellies of cows.

Fucking Vikings.

Word of the massacre had sped across Mull yesterday, then over the water to Oban bay before Helgi's longship had even left the beach. The king in Dunollie had sent Domhnall and some men to investigate.

They had crossed the sound this morning.

Such a beautiful place. Such holy men. Such learning.

It was a place of saints.

Fucking absolute fucking Scandinavians.

Even his pony seemed to buckle at the horror.

Domhnall jumped down and walked towards the ruins where his men and labourers were searching for survivors. A dragon might as well have done this: a giant lizard-beast come up from Hell in a rage, smashing bodies with its tail and breathing fire on the stones. Nothing was left standing. The dormitories, the church, the houses, the farm, the outbuildings and barns: all were roofless and charred. The grain stores were spoiled, the altar was bare, the treasury smashed and empty.

Fourteen of the farm's women had been taken as slaves. A goldsmith, stonemason and parchment maker, too. Domhnall counted the bodies of seventeen farm labourers.

Everything worth anything was gone.

But the worst sight of all was the awful flower of corpses laid out around the cross of Saint John. There, the bodies and heads of the monks lay scattered in a circle where they'd fallen, the white of their robes stained holy red with their blood.

Vikings really are such unbelievable fuckers.

Callum, his bailey, nodded and regarded the bloody yard sadly. What else was there to say?

As Domhnall and Callum drew nearer, they saw the remains of poor Abbot Blathmac: two arms, a leg, a head and a . . . hunk of? . . . laid out in a neat pile in front of the great stone cross. As if an offering.

Dear God, I need to puke.

The latrine's over there, Callum pointed, *but I'd give it a moment.*

Domhnall felt his stomach rise and buck. He stumbled away from the piteous sight and hurried towards the pit. He hadn't even reached the hut before he gave up, fell to his knees on the mud and vomited.

And vomited and vomited and vomited.

Once he was spent, Domhnall lay still in the cool mist.

Domhnall of Crinan was a capable lord in both war and administration. He was a favourite of the king, his cousin, to whom he was utterly loyal, and he had travelled in Europe. He had never seen anything as bereft of pity as this satanic butchery.

Dear God, where are you? he asked himself under his breath. *Where are you in this Hell?*

Now, Domhnall was a good Christian, and he knew that despair was a mortal sin, but nevertheless even he was surprised when he heard, in response to his plaintive doubt, a determined, wobbling voice rise from the earth and sing.

O come, let us sing to the Lord,
Let us make a joyful noise to the rock of our salvation,
Let us come into His presence with thanksgiving,
Let us make a joyful noise to Him with songs of praise.

The plainsong was coming from a shit pit.

★

Domhnall and his men spent the morning checking every house and outbuilding for survivors. The island is small, and so they were able to be thorough. As well as the boy monk who had hidden in the cludgie, there were several women and a handful of children who had managed to flee the scene and hide among the rocks and caves on the far side of the island. Four of the farmhands had survived by playing dead in the stables, and, near the hives on the hill's back, they had found the mead wife attending to her bees.

Her husband had been killed. She had carefully laid his body next to the smithy cottage, which had miraculously survived the torch. She must have spent the night alone. Even the harder men shuddered at the thought of it.

The poor woman couldn't speak. No wonder.

Domhnall arranged the men into work parties. Graves must be dug, dangerous timbers demolished and the survivors and their remaining goods taken down to the boats for evacuation to the mainland.

There was no future here, Domhnall thought. At least, not as a holy place. Northmen were like midges: once they find you, they never leave you alone. The monastery had been on the island since old times, but it was not old times any more. Helgi would be back in the autumn. Hadn't he said so himself? The ploughboy laddie had told them all the story of what happened to Blathmac. Any people left here, any animals, any wealth, would be offered up to the Danes as a blood sacrifice. The king had neither the men nor the ships to defend this thin, odd place. It was hard enough to keep hold of Mull.

No, it was clear to Domhnall that the monastery must be abandoned, the land left to pasture and the survivors taken to Oban, where they could be put to work for the Church.

The men dug three pits: one for the brothers, one for the men and one for the women.

Callum suggested they ought to make a single grave for Abbot Blathmac. He pointed out that he was related to kings and also that, given the manner of his passing, it was possible he would be made a saint.

Domhnall agreed. Feeling pious, he dug the old man's grave himself. He chose a spot overlooking the bay where Helgi's ship had arrived. It was a pretty, sun-dappled spot, beneath a stunted oak.

After he had dug, Domhnall gathered the saint's torn body.

He managed most of it in two trips.

*

By late afternoon the work was done. The last two ferry
boats waited to carry Domhnall, his men and the ponies
over the sound to Fionnphort.

They'd taken whatever meat was salvageable; there was
as yet no harvestable crops. Callum, who knew about these
things, had suggested they leave the sheep and cattle till
later in the year when they had pastured.

Domhnall looked at the shadowed island, lifeless and
hollow behind him. Then, standing watching them from the
rise above the village, he saw the mead wife.

What about her? Domhnall pointed.

She won't come, said Callum. *She wants to stay.*

Bring her here. Domhnall liked plans to be followed. This
was not the plan.

There's no point.

I will determine if there is a point, Callum. Callum was a
talented bailey, but he knew it and liked others to know it,
too. If Callum's mother hadn't been a nurse to the Crinan
men, Domhnall felt Callum would have been beheaded
years ago. He wore his skill like it was jewellery, and that
annoyed people. *Besides, she can speak for herself.*

She can't.

*For God's sake, Callum, just bring the woman here so I can
interrogate her.*

Domhnall, she's mute.

Mute?

Domhnall looked at the mead wife. She was bent over,

feeding her chickens. A tall woman. Her tunic was bright blue and clean. Her face was peasant-tanned. Her white underskirts were stained from the puddles of purple-black blood.

She looked over at Domhnall. She could tell she was being spoken about, he guessed. Her look was calm. Whatever they were talking about, she didn't care.

Did she smile? Domhnall thought she might already be half in the otherworld.

Leave her, he said. *She can attend to the cows.*

*

I also will stay!

Dear God, what now? The cry came from the little shit-boy: the monk who had survived in the latrine, the one the men had taken to calling the stinky miracle.

I will stay!

No, you won't. Domhnall gently shoved him back onto the boat. But the boy pushed back.

I will stay, the boy insisted, his expression unusually fierce.

Why? sighed Domhnall.

It is my duty to serve God and Saint Colm and to honour Abbot Blathmac.

Son, you have no companions.

I will gather companions.

Only suicidal ones. Domhnall's teeth were grinding. The crew on the boats were grumbling. The tide was going out.

The boy stood now, tall on the beach, waving his arms, his crappy cassock flapping about his skinny legs. *God has spared me for a reason!*

What reason?

To save this holy place.

God spared you because you hid in the shitter, Brother Martin. Even the Vikings didn't expect that. That from Callum, and Domhnall had to admit it was funny.

The boy rose angrily and spread his arms like Christ. *I spent a night alone, amongst filth, in the most abandoned place imaginable, with only the Lord beside me. The Lord Jesus kept me strong. In return I made a promise to Him that I would serve Saint Colm. That I would never again abandon my faith in cowardice . . . I will not leave.*

The evening slowly crept over the island. Curlews peeped. Domhnall wanted his dinner.

The king wants the island cleared.

This land belongs to the Church.

Son, you're barely a monk.

My allegiance is to God alone.

Domhnall loved God, but his messengers irritated him. Like all classes of men who didn't fight or work, he found them too fond of their own thought. They spoke as if everything they said was a newly minted coin worth passing from hand to hand, their voices rising and falling the same way they sang their plainsong – up and down and on and on.

Do what you like. The mead wife can feed you. It's a matter for the Church.

Domhnall signalled to the men. They pushed the boats onto the ebbing tide, jumped aboard and drifted away into the gathering night.

★

The island was silent.

The moon rose, full and fat. Moonbeams gilded the flowers and vegetables in the abandoned garden. Warm light filled the smithy window.

From the ruined church, a lonely bell rang Evensong.

Clang! Clang! Clang! Clang! Clang!

Chapter 3

Fuck, I could do with a drink.

Grimur couldn't face opening his eyes. A drum beat of pain thumped at the front of his skull. His tongue was dry and sticky. He felt sick and weak.

I had so much mead.

He could taste it in the back of his throat, mixed with pre-sick: acid and herby, but still with an actually quite delicious overtone of soft honey.

Ladle after ladle he had drunk from the deep oak barrel. Each hornful seemed better than the last. The more the mead wife poured, the more he drank. The more he drank, the more he felt his sadness turn to warmth, his tiredness to energy, his anxiety to hope.

That was then.

This was now.

Now, Grimur felt anxious, sad and tired. His body was seeped full of filth, regret and despair. He should have killed her. If he'd killed her, he wouldn't have drunk so much. He'd been so close to killing her. If only she hadn't made him laugh.

But she did.

And he was, at least, cosy in his bed. Smell of soft earth and grass. He could stay here for ever . . .

But, no, he had to move! Wake up, meet the others, wherever they were, and get back to the ship for the journey to Shetland. They wouldn't wait for him. He had to move.

I have to move.

I have to move.

One, two, three, move.

One, two, three . . .

One . . .

Grimur regathered his faltering will.

One. Two. Three. MOVE!

With a roar he opened his eyes and tried to sit up in bed. But he couldn't. In fact, he couldn't move at all. He seemed to be bound into something. Was he tangled up in bedclothes? He wasn't sure, and he couldn't be sure because – and this was the other worrying thing – he couldn't see anything.

His eyes were open, but he could take in only utter darkness. Had he gone blind?

Grimur wriggled and pushed his body, wriggled and pushed. His heart began to race. Finally, he managed to move his left hand.

He realised he was holding a knife. He tried to saw through whatever hellish bonds held him. He wiggled his hand from side to side, using the knife to gouge and cut. As he moved, he felt cool grains of soft earth roll down into his sleeve.

Earth.

Grimur's whole body fell limp, and his mind was flooded in utter horror.

He was buried in earth.

But I am not dead, he thought. I am not dead.

He spoke the words out loud. *I am not dead! I AM NOT DEAD!*

He spoke and he spoke . . . but he was not heard.

*

The day dawned clear and cool, the smell of death and smoke blown away, at last, by a good westerly wind. The birds were returning to the fruit trees in the orchard. This morning the rooster had crowed just after the clang of the monastery bell.

If the mead wife had closed her eyes, the day might just have felt like any other. But this was not a day like any other. This was her first day alone.

But since, alone or with others, one's work cannot remain undone, the mead wife did not spend much time considering the implications of her new situation beyond noticing that she had slept particularly well last night. She rose, washed, fed the chickens, left milk for the cat and set out to find the herbs for the mead of May.

On the street, she passed the boy monk, who was singing the Office of the Dead over the graves of the brothers.

Come, let us sing to the Lord,
And shout with joy to the Rock who saves us.
Let us approach him with praise and thanksgiving,
And sing joyful songs to the Lord.

He looked like a child in costume. His silly bald head was growing back hair. His eyes were wild and lost. But his voice was strong.

Hunger and shock had filled Martin with transcendent empathy. He was God's servant, his body merely an expression of God's will on earth, a vessel filled with light and grace and – yes! yes! – the Holy Spirit.

Martin would feel no grief for his brothers, who were so surely one with bliss! No, Martin was going to visit every single grave on the island and sing the proper Offices over every one with passion, faith and love.

A child, really.

The mead wife decided to bring him porridge later, and a clean cassock.

*

Grimur slowed his breathing in an effort to quell the rising panic. Taking in his situation, he realised that, although he had been buried, something wooden had been laid across his face and chest, and so there was, at least, a small space into which he could breathe.

He took a moment to check he wasn't dreaming.

Then he thrashed his body with all the force he could muster. Though he was swaddled in earth like an infant bound, he kicked his legs, arched his back, pushed his shoulders, butted his head . . . Every muscle in his body strained. Had he dislodged any space? Maybe? A little.

Breathless, panting, sweating, he gathered his strength and thrashed once more. He felt, for a moment, so fuelled by total fear that all the strength of his youth returned to him. He strained, pushed, twitched, kicked and punched, using every muscle, every limb.

I will not die here.

He used the knife in his left hand to cut and dig. The earth above the knife was softened. He managed to flex his wrist up and down. Sensing progress, he bunched his hand into a fist with the knife at its head and twisted, drilled and thrust the knife upwards.

I will not die here.

Another moment of recovery, another swelling tide of panic, another quelling breath.

Push, twist, gouge, reverse, push, twist, gouge, reverse, push, twist, gouge, reverse.

I will not die here.

*

Brother Martin was tired. He had not slept well. He had not really slept at all. He carried a flagon of whisky, which he had fetched from a dark corner of the broken pantry store. As he sang, he sipped. He felt it give him strength.

*The Lord is God, the mighty God, the great King over all
    the gods.*

He holds in His hands the depths of the Earth and the
highest mountains as well.
He made the sea; it belongs to Him, the dry land, too, for
it was formed by His hands.

Martin stepped over the broken monastery gate and headed along the path towards the bay. The fresh wind enlivened his spirits. Singing filled him with hope. A ewe nursed her newborn lamb on a daisy-strewn patch of machair.

Come, then, let us bow down and worship, bending the
knee before the Lord, our maker,
For He is our God and we are His people, the flock He
shepherds.

Martin's morning task was nearly complete.

One grave left.

One more litany from the Office of the Dead.

*

Push, twist, gouge, reverse, push, twist, gouge, reverse, push, twist, gouge, reverse.

Breathe . . . breathe . . . breathe . . . breathe.

Push, twist, gouge, reverse, push, twist, gouge, reverse, push, twist, gouge, reverse.

Breathe . . . breathe . . . breathe . . . breathe.

Push, twist, gouge, reverse, push, twist, gouge, reverse, push, twist, gouge, reverse.

Breathe . . . breathe . . . breathe . . . breathe.

*

A simple stone on top of disturbed earth marked this last grave. On the stone were scratched some runes. Martin could not read them, but he knew they meant the grave belonged to a raider.

A murderer.

A horrible slaughterer.

A plunderer.

A rapist.

A satanic pagan destroyer of good.

And yet, Martin thought, with a slight surge of Christian pride, a soul.

A soul made by God who deserved the correct liturgy, if this island was to remain a sacred place.

Martin mustered all his piety, took a drink of whisky and, to an audience of uncaring terns, he spoke these words:

> *All who are in their graves shall hear the voice of the Son*
> *of God;*
> *— those who have done good deeds will go forth to the*
> *resurrection of life;*
> *those who have done evil will go forth to the resurrection*
> *of judgment.*
> *In an instant, in the twinkling of an eye, at the final*
> *trumpet blast, the dead shall rise.*
> *— those who have done good deeds will go forth to the*
> *resurrection of life;*
> *those who have done evil will go forth to the resurrection*
> *of judgment.*

Martin bowed his head solemnly, the terns rose onto the breeze and a hand thrust up through the soil and waggled its fingers like a disgusting, terrifying flower.

A hand.

A human hand.

*

Grimur's heart leapt.

Air! He had broken through, by Odin! The world was only a foot of soft, fresh, new-dug earth above him. Whoever had buried him had not put themselves to a great deal of effort.

He flexed his hand. Stretched it. Splayed it.

Then Grimur felt something he had not expected. Another hand. Another hand touched his, and held it, gently, and shook it.

A greeting.

Grimur wept. His body flooded with joy. He would not die here!

Grimur let out a mighty roar from the very depths of his being – a formless bellow, a guttural heart song, a mighty shout of life – and thrust his other hand up through the soil.

Chapter 4

The grinning, bearded, wild-eyed face of a Viking stared up from the open grave.

Unsure of what to say, Martin played it safe. *Good morning.*

Good morning to you, the corpse replied in Gaelic but with a strong Northman's accent. *Would you mind giving me a hand out of here?*

His arms reached ghoulishly upwards.

Mustering his courage, Martin pulled. The dead man got to his feet, stepped out of the grave, brushed the dirt from his tunic and shook the earth out of his boots.

As he did so, Martin tried to make sense of recent events.

There had been a massacre. He had, to his shitty-shame, hid from martyrdom. Afterwards, he had gone to pray at the fresh graves. Just now, at this one grave, a soul, it would seem, had been brought back from the dead.

With dawning awe, Martin realised. *It's a miracle!* He jumped and clapped. *It's a miracle! It's a miracle! Alleluia!*

It's not a miracle, son, it's a mix-up. The dead man put his cold arm around Martin's shoulder in a friendly way and pointed to the stone flagon. *Is that whisky?*

Martin nodded.

The cadaver took the jar and drank.

And drank again. And again. And again.

Then he wiped his lips and smiled. *Truly, you are the son of God!*

He kissed his saviour.

What's your name, Godfish?

Martin hesitated. *I am Martin, Brother Martin, of the monastery of* I.

Brother Martin of the monastery of I, *you've given me back my life. I'm in your debt. As soon as I'm back in my own hall, I'll make offerings to your god: cow, horse, sheep, lamb, slave — or all five of them, whichever you think best. But, for now, if you want me to live, the best thing you can do is forget you ever saw me. Leave now. Go back to your church. Tell no one what happened here. Do you understand? The sooner I get away from* I, *the better it will be for both of us.*

Martin was disappointed. He had hoped for a rather more biblical denouement to this, his first resurrection, but he couldn't deny that the corpse had made a clear request, and he didn't want to argue with the undead.

I understand. He offered his hand. *Well, it was nice to meet you.*

It was nice to meet you, too.

The man's hand was warm. Martin held it tight, for a moment, and looked him in the eye. *Friend . . . if you ever feel hungry or cold or lonely, come . . . come to the church. We will take you in.*

The revenant nodded. *I won't.*

Martin bade goodbye and made his way back along the soft peat path to the smoking ruins of the village. Despite his urge, he was very careful not to look back, lest his doubt somehow turn the poor man to salt.

*

Grimur scanned the island. The beach was empty. Helgi's ship had long gone. No sign of any locals either. He was alone.

He turned to his grave and examined the goods with which they'd buried him: a knife, his axe, some string and a bowl.

What? No sword? No silver? No woman? No horse?

Not even a chicken?

Grimur was hurt. If he had actually died, he'd be walking into Valhalla with his hair unkempt, no coins, no coat and quite without sparkle. He noticed some scratched runes on the cobble they'd placed at his head as a marker.

Here lies Grimur No-Name, not a bad guy.

Not a bad guy?

Grimur looked inside his helmet.

His comb. At least they had left him his comb.

He ran the fine bone teeth through his hair and pulled

out tangles, twigs and soil. Then he straightened out his beard and rolled his moustache ends. Finally, he tightened his belt, sucked in his belly, slapped his face, adjusted his cock so it looked a bit bigger in his britches and barked out a jovial *ho!*

Barefoot on the soft machair, he kicked and stretched his limbs and beat his chest.

Good morning, life, you gorgeous bitch – I'm back!

That felt better.

*

The grass of *I* is rich and green. It's a pleasure to walk on. You could eat it yourself if you had the right teeth. Whoever they were, these Christ-loving men, they keep their cows well, Grimur thought.

He was going to have to hide out for a few days before he went looking for a boat. He didn't want to be on the mainland so soon after the raid. Even at the best of times, no one was less welcome in Scotland than a Viking after a massacre.

Grimur explored the northern shore until he found a sheltered overhang which would do for a camp. A small colony of seals basked in the sun on the rocks below.

Grimur liked seals. He enjoyed it when they swam alongside the ship. They sped through the water like thoughts following an idea. His father once told him seals carried the souls of women.

He could probably catch a seal with a spear. He could

probably carve a spear from a sapling or, better, some timber from the burnt cottages. He could probably walk over to the cottages now, steal some timbers and see what he could catch. He probably ought to move. Once the tide was up, the seals would be gone. He had a very long journey ahead of him to find his way back to Helgi's hall in Shetland. He would need food. Seal meat dried well. You could chew it as you went along.

The first part of the journey, through the kingdom of Dál Riata, he should be able to make at good speed. He could move during the daytime. As a lone man with an axe, he would have to be discreet but, through his father, who had been born in Ireland, he spoke sufficient Gaelic to pass, if he mumbled.

But then he'd have to cross Pictland, and Grimur had no Pictish, not even 'hello'. In fact, he knew nothing about Picts, their country, its routes, its customs or kings. He'd have to travel at night, without fire, hiding at all times, and that would slow him down.

Then, if he made it to the north coast, he'd have to make a boat or steal one. Those were hard waters in a longship, never mind a coracle or a canoe.

It would take him maybe twenty days to get to Thurso. Twenty-five? Thirty? What if he got lost? Thirty-five? Forty, to be safe.

He'd get ten days' meat from a seal, maybe. Could he steal food? Too many questions. No, it was risky enough to travel across unknown country, never mind be hunted as a thief.

Why did Helgi have to be such a prick? Tearing an abbot apart with horses was such a typical Helgi move. If anyone within a dozen miles caught him now, he'd be skinned alive.

Grimur didn't want to be skinned alive. Of all the possible deaths, it was definitely his least favourite. Previously it would have been being buried alive, but now he'd experienced that and discovered it was not too bad.

A bee buzzed around his face. The sun was warm. Below him, the seals called out their sad cries. Grimur didn't want to eat women.

He would need to think.

The soft suck of the waves at the cobbled beach seemed to say to him *shh . . . shh . . . shh . . .*

He lay back in the sun. The machair smelt sweet on the breeze. He closed his eyes.

Shh . . . shh . . . shh . . .

Chapter 5

Without shepherds, more lambs than usual would die that May. Half a dozen little white bodies lay scattered across the machair already. Crows were going to get fat on the carrion through the slowly lengthening days. The mingled smell of death and spring grass was going to become revolting eventually, but, fortunately, there would be no one there to smell it.

*

Martin was determined to make up for his humiliation. He had decided he would keep to the monastery offices and honour God with all the correct devotions, despite the fact that he was now the only monk left on *I*.

He began, again, to observe the Holy Liturgy of the Hours.

*

Matins

Waking from a broken sleep, Martin sat on the stone bench at the back of the church and shivered. After some time, he lit a candle on what had been the altar but which was now just slabs of smashed marble. Facing the guttering light, he chanted:

Today salvation has come to the world.
Let us sing to Him who rose from the dead,
The author of our lives,
Having destroyed death by death,
He has given us victory,
And great mercy.

On still nights, the plainchant of the monks at Matins would float across the Sound of Mull and farm wives would listen to it as they lay awake beside their sleeping men.

Not tonight.

Tonight, these halting gasps barely travelled across the yard.

Lauds

A grey dawn light crept under the broken door of the church. Martin blinked awake. Why was the stone floor unswept? Why was the altar in pieces? Where was the Father Abbot?

And then he remembered.

They were all dead.

He staggered to his feet, called and responded:

I called with all my heart: Lord, hear me.
— I called with all my heart: Lord, hear me.
I will keep Your commandments.
— I called with all my heart: Lord, hear me.

*Glory be to the Father and to the Son and to the Holy
    Spirit.*
— I called with all my heart: Lord, hear me.

Not called: whispered. Not responded: mouthed.

Prime

The sun was fully risen, though in the pale colours of
morning, you would hardly have noticed. Martin stood
facing the big stone cross of Saint Martin in the yard.

*Whoever wishes to be saved must, above all, keep the Catholic
faith. For unless a person keeps this faith whole and entire, he will
undoubtedly be lost for ever . . .*

His knees kept buckling.

The mead wife brought him some broth. She put the
bowl in his hands. He drank. The warmth filled him.

Terce

The afternoon was bright and warm, and Martin was dozing
on the grass. Gently, the mead wife shook his shoulder. He
jerked awake, sat upright and sang out loudly:

I lift up my eyes to the hills!
To find deliverance!
From the Lord deliverance comes to me!
The Lord who made Heaven and Earth!
Never will He who guards thee allow my foot to stumble!
Never fall asleep at his post!

This time she brought porridge.

He scooped up spoon after spoon of milky oats. She smiled as she watched him eat. He sucked the wooden spoon. He raised the bowl to his face and licked. He was not a monk but a hungry boy, and though his soul's light was dim, the mead wife could see each mouthful gave him strength.

He gave her back the bowl.

As he did so, he looked at her with an expression of such loss, such bewilderment and pain, that she felt it in herself.

Sext

Normally, in the afternoon, the monks of *I* would devote themselves to practical tasks.

Today being dry, the season being spring, Martin decided he would work in the kitchen garden.

The mead wife fed her hens and watched.

The vegetable beds had been torn up by the hooves of frightened cattle and horses during the raid. Martin patiently gathered up the damaged produce and laid it out in rows on the spoiled ground. Then he knelt down with soil in his hand. Carefully, he put handfuls of soil over each one of the smashed vegetables. Was he trying to replant them? Or bury them? After he had covered one with soil, he patted the earth down with a trowel, then he kneel-crawled along the row to the next smashed turnip or broken kale stalk and did the same thing again.

As he worked, he sang:

*Give thanks to the Lord, the Lord is gracious, His mercy
    endures for ever.
Give thanks to the Lord, the Lord is gracious, His mercy
    endures for ever.
Give thanks to the Lord, the Lord is gracious, His mercy
    endures for ever.*

His voice was stronger now. He climbed around the notes randomly but with confidence.

Perhaps he thought he had the power to make dead things grow.

*

A shower passed, then breeze, then sun again.

The mead wife strode across the rough field to the hollow where she kept her hives. The broom was just beginning to show its yellow flowers. A dozen mud-covered conical skeps sat neatly in rows on the rough grass. She wore her bee hood, a long-necked snood with a woven basket covering her face, as she lay pats of smouldering cow dung on the ground.

The bees filled the air with a drowsy hum.

Morning, ladies! (With bees, it was important to be respectful.) *Sorry I've been away. Things have been a wee bit lively lately in the world of men.*

Carefully, she opened up the first skep.

Nothing for you to worry about.

She peered inside.

Nothing for you to worry about at all.

The bees crawled happily round their complex interior architecture. The honeyed combs were like carved ivory screens flooded with warm summer sunlight. The mead wife smiled. She was proud of these women workers whom she'd helped through the hungry months with barley cakes and mead.

Brother Finnian thought bees were male. That's what his books told him. She had never contradicted him, but she'd always known better. She'd tasted the bitter acrid stuff that comes out of male bodies, and she'd tasted the sweet nourishing stuff that comes out of female bodies. Honey was a woman's gift, that much was clear.

Also, bees lived together without fighting, sang as a choir and worked all year round. To say nothing of the fact that they spent their lives serving the needs of a big fat lazy king.

Women.

Good work, sisters.

She dipped her pinky into one of the combs, curled out a golden glob and tasted: pine, wine, sea, peat, dandelion, a little fermented apple . . . some bitterness, maybe a trace of regret.

Not a trace of massacre.

She'd been worried it might have been spoiled by the violence. She'd half-expected it to taste of smoke or pain. But, no, the sisters seemed to have avoided the worst of it. This was good. She'd be able to start on the new season's beer straight away.

She sucked her finger happily.

Woman?

The voice startled her.

Woman, ho!

She turned and saw a Viking. Black hair, grey beard, pot belly, scar and, on his hip, a killing axe.

Have you got any more of that mead?

It was the man who had killed her husband.

*

The last time she'd seen this man, she'd knocked him senseless with a draught of her Felling Brew: the strongest mead she had. The drink left him lying unconscious on the smithy floor, and she'd taken her chance to run. By the time she came back, he'd been taken to the boat by his comrades.

Now he was standing in front of her.

It's the best I ever tasted.

He smiled and held his hands out in supplication.

After a moment, she nodded.

She put the honey shelf back in the hive and beckoned him follow her over the moor.

Chapter 6

Nones

The day drew to its close in a late flowering bloom. The falling sun gave the sea a metallic bronze patina. Martin sang to himself as he walked the northern beaches alone.

I will praise You, Lord my God, with all my heart;
I will glorify Your name forever.
For great is Your love toward me;
You have delivered me from the depths,
from the realm of the dead.

The hills of Mull seemed, to him, as sharp and green as if they'd been drawn by Brother Baithéne himself.

*

The mead wife cut a hunk of mutton on the wooden board. Grimur sat on the bench and fed the fire. He'd carried some kelp and nettles to throw in the pot. It was warm in the cottage. He couldn't help but notice the black stains on the table from where the smith's blood had seeped into the wood.

As she chopped, she hummed a tune:

> *Late it was, I saw last night,*
> *A red cape on the hill above,*
> *My heart it leapt at every step,*
> *I thought that it was you, my love.*

Grimur sang along quietly as he poked the fire. As he sang, she stared at him, thinking, how the fuck does a Viking know the words to my mother's song?

Grimur didn't notice her staring. He was too hungry and too sleepy, and he was enjoying the silent dance of the flames. After a while the barley softened in the stock. The meat was brown. The mead wife brought out two wooden bowls; they dipped them in the stew and ate together by the firelight.

He was a big man. His belly hung over his belt. His arms were covered in light ginger hair, but the hair on his head was still black. His skin was brown, like sweet cheese. His eyes were blue.

She took his drinking horn and filled it from a jar.

He drank.

He drank again.

He burped a murmur of low appreciation, like a post-coital bull, and gave her back the empty horn. *Thank you.*

When he'd killed the smith, he'd seemed to her like a wild bear, but now he was a different animal: placid, alone.

Mead wife, he asked, *what's your name?*

She hesitated. The mead wife hadn't spoken to anyone,

woman or man, for over ten years. Not since the smith broke her jaw that day during her first pregnancy.

After a moment she said: *Una.*

He took her hand. He gripped it. He smiled. *Fucking great dinner, Una.*

Glowing, he turned back to face the fire.

Vespers

Night was falling. The church was dark. Martin's voice was quiet as he lit a candle for every soul lost in the massacre . . . for Brother Baithéne, Brother Gavin, Brother Fergus, Brother Colman, Brother Michael, Brother Clochán, Brother Ninian, Brother Jerome, Brother Odhran, Brother Colm, Brother Adomnán, Brother Peter, Brother Declan, Brother Tristan, Brother Ciaran, Brother Aodhan, Brother Flann, Brother Taghd, Brother Niall, Brother Cobtach, Brother Muirchertach, Brother Bran, Brother Rónán, Brother Máel Dúin, Brother Crundmáel, Brother Finnian, Father Abbot Blathmac.

O God the Father, Creator of the world,
Have mercy on the souls of the faithful departed.

O God the Son, Redeemer of mankind,
Deliver the souls of the faithful departed,

O God the Holy Ghost, perfector of the elect,
Accomplish the bliss of the faithful departed.

Slowly, the church filled with light.

*

The Viking slept on cow straw by the fire. Una lay in the cot.

She felt she ought to weep, but she wasn't sure why. She was happy her husband was dead. She was sad about the monks. She was happy the bees had survived the winter. She was worried about Brother Martin. She felt sorry for the Viking, so far away from home. She was happy he liked her mead.

She would never have wept in front of the smith. In eleven years of marriage, she had given him nothing. But the smith was gone now.

She thought of her three children living on Mull with her sister-in-law. She thought of the two she'd buried on *I*. At every one of those partings, she'd fought to keep her eyes dry.

Now, the weight of it all was a dam in her, and she wanted it to break.

Compline

The night was calm and clear.

> *Lord, now let Your servant depart in peace,*
> *For I have seen Your salvation,*
> *Which You prepared in sight of everyone,*
> *To be a light to the gentiles.*
> *and a glory to the people of Israel.*

Martin's voice, a pure tenor plainchant, moving naturally over the melody like a burn over stones, carried out from the church, across the flagstone yard and out into the star-speckled darkness.

> *Glory be to the Father, and to the Son,*
> *and to the Holy Ghost;*
> *as it was in the beginning,*
> *is now, and ever shall be*
> *world without end.*
> *Amen.*

Una heard the song. She cried.

Chapter 7

Grimur sat on what was left of the monastery wall and drank his mead from a clay cup, quite the Christian man about town.

He considered his situation.

If he was going to make his way back to Shetland, he'd have to leave soon. The moon would be full in a day or so. Then it would be a good time to travel.

This was his plan: tomorrow he'd slap the boy monk and make him reveal some likely whereabouts for the saint's silver reliquary. Then he'd go digging. Once he found the treasure, he'd take some food from the woman's stores, pinch a couple of big skins of drink, steal the monastery boat and row till he found a safe place to put in on the mainland.

It was a good plan.

Big swells rolled down the sound, great sea slabs shifting. The storms of yesterday were revealing themselves in the water today.

Wait till the swells calm, maybe.

Next moon.

★

Clang! Clang! Clang!

The broken bell rang out across the island.

Martin processed around the big stone cross of Saint John. As he did so, he chanted, his robes billowing out behind him in the blowy morning.

It was heroic really, thought Grimur, this task the boy had set himself: to build a new monastery in the ruins of the old. Of course, it was bound to fail. At any moment, a lone bandit with a coracle could row over from Mull and take him for a slave. The nearest king was two days' ride away and hadn't shown a great deal of desire to protect the church anyway.

The boy fought against the gusts, determined, almost joyful.

It was funny.

Grimur went inside.

★

There is no boat.

What do you mean there is no boat?

All the boats were taken by Domhnall of Crinan when he evacuated the island.

They must have left a boat for the boy priest?

Una shrugged.

He said he didn't want one. He said it would be temptation.

Didn't they leave a boat for you?

Why would they leave a boat for me?

Grimur's face fell.

Fuck.

Una laughed.

What?

What do you call a Viking without a boat? said Una.

I don't know.

Dead.

That's not funny.

*

The porridge bubbled. Una slopped some into a wooden bowl. She added a drip of her spring honey to give it a bit more life. Brother Martin was reviving well. She was pleased the monastery would continue. Una wasn't interested in God, or in worlds beyond this one, but she did like singing and she liked men not killing people. She felt it might make more sense for them to worship their creator by farming, or fishing, or gardening, but if they wanted to do it by living together and singing about matters beyond all understanding, then who was she to stop them.

But Una knew it wasn't prayer bringing that boy back to life.

It was porridge.

Give me that. This was Grimur, now.

It's for the priest!

He reached across from the bench and took the bowl.

I'll take it to him.

Grimur strolled across the yard to the ruins, dipping his bread in the porridge as he went.

*

There was no sign of the boy. Not by the cross, nor in the kitchen garden. The refectory was empty save for a lost ewe which must have wandered in. The dormitory roof had half fallen through. No one was in the stable. The grain barn had been burned down entirely.

The porridge was cooling.

Behind the church, near the monastery wall, on a small rise, Grimur saw there was an unburnt building which he hadn't noticed before: a long low hut facing south.

He went inside.

It took a moment for his eyes to adjust. It was a clean whitewashed single room with a long wooden workbench along the wall. Above the bench, daylight came in through a thin window. Thick candlesticks were placed along the table, emerging like pillars out of formless wax heaps. Stools sat at intervals. Around the room Grimur noticed various boxes, jars and a scattering of small hand-held tools which were clearly intended for doing some kind of fine close work.

But that wasn't the thing.

None of that was the thing.

The thing – the thing which flooded Grimur's attention as he took in the room – was the colour.

The colour!

The workbench was covered with smears of bright blue, red, yellow and green. Sheets of illustrated parchment were tacked to the wall with pictures of multicoloured birds, golden suns, bright green forests, black cats, purple emperors and white horses. Dozens of small pots full of bright powders lay on shelves.

Everywhere Grimur's eye landed he saw some flash, some splash, some daub of colour.

And, in the middle of it all, on a small table, he noticed a large pale leather-bound object, about the size of a buckler shield, square, boxy and thick. It lay in a shaft of bright daylight, as if it had been placed there deliberately.

Grimur opened the lid.

*

Imagine a falcon, looking down on a jarl's garden in winter. A golden wall surrounds the garden and also divides it in two, neatly down the middle. The top of the wall is studded with colourful jewels: ruby, amber, blue john and quartz. The stones sparkle and catch the light.

On one side of the garden, dozens of black pine martens form patterns in the bright white snow: playing, fighting, dancing, twisting. Beside them, six large red and green serpents curl and twist. Perhaps the martens are their prey.

On the other side of the thin golden wall live three great beasts: an eagle, a calf and a royal lion. These beasts are guarded by a shepherd with wings.

The beasts are calm. The shepherd is content.

★

Don't touch the book!

Martin's voice shocked Grimur from his dream and he threw the porridge bowl up in the air. Globs of sticky oats scattered through the room like snow.

No!

Mess landed everywhere.

No! No! No!

Martin leapt to clean the box. He gathered the hem of his cassock and used it as a cloth. Grimur saw now that the object was not, in fact, a box but instead a bound pile of parchment sheaves. Each flattened sheet was covered in tightly packed writing and coloured illustrations. Grimur had never seen so much writing. It was like a waterfall.

What did you do that for?! Martin was furious.

I'm sorry. You surprised me.

The boy monk wasn't listening. He was frantically wiping oat gloop off the soft leather cover of the thing he had called 'a book'.

It's only porridge.

I thought you'd gone home.

I decided not to.

Because you wanted to destroy more of God's own property?

No.

What then?

Nothing. I just . . . I need a place to stay and . . .

And?

. . . you said I would always be welcome.

Martin stopped. He had said that. It was a fair point.

I was bringing you food. I'm staying with the mead wife. You saved my life. I wondered if perhaps there was some way I could be useful . . .

The Viking seemed sincere.

. . . to pay my debt?

To God?

To you.

★

Martin turned each parchment page very slowly and very carefully.

We call it 'The Book of I'. It's a copy of the Holy Gospels of Matthew, Mark, Luke and John. The king in Armagh commissioned it to celebrate the life of Saint Colm, who founded this house. This book is the last Gospel. The Gospel of John.

What does this say?

Martin sounded out the words in Latin. *'In principio erat Verbum et Verbum erat apud Deum et Deus erat Verbum.'*

Is that Frankish?

Latin.

What does it say?

It says: 'In the beginning was the Word, and the Word was with God, and the Word was God.'

I don't understand.

Well, it takes many years and much guidance to understand these words.

Do you understand it?

Well, I wouldn't say I know it completely, but it's something like 'Everything is a story, a story told by God, and the story is God' . . . At least that's how Brother Aed explained it to me.

Everything is a story told by a god.

Sort of.

Like the strange sisters who sit under the tree and weave our fate?

No, not like that at all. I don't know who those sisters are, but this is a very different thing. This was written by a man who actually knew God. A man who was amongst the first of his disciples.

Was he an Irishman?

He was a Jew, which means he was a Hebrew. All the first followers of Jesus were Hebrew, but they wrote their Gospels in Greek, though they are written here in Latin . . .

Grimur nodded, but he didn't understand anything Martin said. He was lost in the pictures. He stopped hearing the boy's voice and instead let his mind fill with serpents, devils, birds, fish, dolphins and trees.

. . . Before the massacre, Brother Rónán, Brother Máel Dúin, Brother Crundmáel and Brother Finnian and Brother Baithéne worked on the book. I and other young ones were novice scribes . . .

Martin was still talking.

. . . the last three chapters are unfinished. Sadly, your comrades killed all my teachers, and their skills died with them, so the book must remain undone . . .

The overgrown meadow outside was alive with larks

and lapwings, carolling and chanting to the bright morning sky.

Martin shut the book.

It's nearly Prime. I've spent too long in here with you. I must work.

No.

No?

Grimur took the monk's hand in his. *Your work is the book.*

Martin broke away and made his way back to the church.

Grimur hurried after him. *You have to finish it.*

I'm only a novice.

Who else will do it?

Whomsoever God wills. I don't have time.

You have all the hours of a long summer's day, implored Grimur.

I need to fix the church.

I'll fix the church.

Where will I sleep?

I'll build you a bed in the writing room.

I don't need a bed.

You need a warm place to sleep.

I'm safe in the church.

You'll catch cold from the stone.

God will guide me!

Does God know how to lay a roof timber? Does God know how to repair thatch?

God knows all things.

When is he planning the works? Does he have the tools? Who are his labourers?

Martin was indignant. *God works through me!*

You said yourself, you're a novice! The Northman blocked the door of the church.

Martin couldn't push past.

You stupid boy. Grimur spoke gently. *Why don't you see? This is your fate. Woven into your story.*

Martin hung his head. He was so tired.

You brought me back from the dead. 'A miracle', you called it. And you were right. I, Grimur No-Name, have been sent back from death to protect you while you finish this book. Even a pagan like me can see that. This task is given to you by your god.

He let the boy go. *Write. The mead wife and I will do everything else.*

At that moment, a long skein of burnt-black geese passed noisily overhead. As they flew, they arranged themselves into something that looked like a raggedy cross.

Chapter 8

Grimur spent the rest of May and early June making the church watertight. He cannibalised roof timbers and salvaged thatch. He used the tools in the carpenter's workshop to cut and shape wood.

When Grimur was growing up, his father did the repair work on Fat Eye's farm in Ålesund. Fat Eye wasn't interested in repair. He liked destruction. That's why he had so many slaves. Fat Eye's slaves performed the dull labour of working the estate, while Fat Eye spent his year raiding, warring and politicking up and down the coast of Norway. He once told Grimur that the only purpose of a man was to fight, fuck and sail ships.

Grimur's father taught him the uses of trees. He showed him which wood was good for boats, which for bows, which for burning and which for building. He showed him how to make and repair all the things necessary for a farm.

Grimur liked repairing.

*

During the long days of light, Martin worked in the scriptorium, copying and illustrating the last three chapters of the *Gospel of John the Apostle*.

Copying was not a simple act of reproduction. It was also a type of prayer, the way to a deeper understanding of scripture. Writing out lines was a meditation on meanings and hidden meanings. Illustrations appeared on the page in a dream state of grace.

Before the massacre, Martin had been apprenticed to blind Brother Aed. Brother Aed was Martin's *anamchara*, his spiritual guide. During winter, when Martin's job was to make candles and do the stinking work of preparing calfskin to make parchment, Aed would discuss with him the lines of the Gospel and their many meanings.

In summer, when the light was good, Martin would sit beside Aed and copy those same lines over and over again to develop his hand.

Without his *anamchara*, Martin could form the letters, but how could he know if he truly understood the text?

It was a puzzle.

He would simply have to trust in God.

*

On some days, after Terce, Grimur and Martin would sit together at the foot of the cross of Saint John, look out over the sound and discuss their work.

One day, Martin told Grimur the story of *I* . . .

Two centuries ago, Saint Colm, who was then a well-known and very holy man, became tired of Ireland and went looking for a new place to found a house. This was to be somewhere from where he could send out missions to pagans and gather souls for Christ, as well as do the work of the Lord with prayer and writing.

So, Saint Colm and his twelve brothers took to the sea in their currachs and let the wind blow them where it would. Well, the wind blew them to I. They landed on the cobbled beach, and Saint Colm said to his brothers: 'This is the right place.'

Then he climbed Dùn Ì and turned his back on Ireland for ever.

The saint and the brothers built on I a new Jerusalem. He performed many miracles. For example, he opened locked doors, he subdued a bear, he foretold of future events, he defeated wizards and he brought the Picts to Christ. They also made together many manuscripts of the Gospels and other holy books. Saint Colm lit the fire of God here. Since then, that fire has never gone out, and if the Lord gives me strength, it never will.

Many abbots followed Saint Colm, and many of them were saints themselves and some founded sister houses in Tiree, in Durrow, in Kells and on Lindisfarne, as well as many other places. You might have heard of Saint Adomnán, who formulated the Law of the Innocents, which asks warriors not to murder women and children but only to kill men in battle?

Grimur hadn't heard of that saint, clearly.

Twenty-one years ago, the Northmen attacked for the first time. I wasn't here then. I wasn't born then. Four dragon ships fell on the monastery, stole everything and took the brothers as slaves.

Then they came again, a few years later, and did the same thing.

And again, a few years later, they did the same thing.

After that last massacre, Muiredach mac Ainbcellaig, the king in Kilmartin, told the Abbot Cellach that he could no longer protect the brothers of I. So, Cellach gathered what was left of their treasures – the library, the silver crosses, the relics and the stores – and prepared to take them all to Kells, where they could be defended by the kings of Tara.

However, on the eve of their departure, one young monk, who was called Brother Blathmac, was visited by Saint Colm in a dream. The saint touched Blathmac on the mouth with his right finger and told him: 'Brother, you will die for I.'

At the time, there had been some dispute about the meaning of this dream. Did I mean Saint Colm? Or the island? The monastery? Or God?

For some days the brothers debated. Finally, Father Abbot Cellach settled the matter by commanding Blathmac and twelve others to stay and rebuild the monastery in a small way, while the others would go to Kells and safety.

Before they left they disarticulated Saint Colm's holy finger bone from the rest of his holy skeleton and put it in a silver reliquary, which Blathmac placed on the altar in the church.

Abbot Blathmac rebuilt the monastery. He repopulated the farm. He welcomed new monks and gathered donations from the wealthy of Argyll. During this time, Saint Colm's finger protected the brothers from plague, crop failure, storm and high politics.

Until this spring, when a red sail was seen on the horizon,

Brother Finnian rang the bell and Abbot Blathmac understood that Saint Colm's prediction had come true.

Abbot Blathmac took a spade, climbed Dùn Ì, dug a pit and placed the bone in the ground.

★

Grimur chewed some old bread. *He buried it on Dùn Ì?*

Yes.

Why didn't he just give the reliquary to Helgi and spare you all the massacre?

Columba's bones make Ì a holy place.

One finger?

Not just any finger – a finger which pored over the words of God, a finger which subdued beasts, blessed waves and held the hands of the poor.

Did he never pick his nose or wipe his arse?

Martin winced at Grimur's vulgarity.

Is it a magic finger?

I wouldn't say it was magic, but it can perform miracles.

What miracles?

When the saint's whole body was here, the effect of the bones was more powerful. Harvests flourished, women became impregnated, sick children were healed, pagan invaders were defeated in battle – but that was all before my time. Since I've been here, we've only had the finger. The finger performs mostly miracles of the heart, such as bad men becoming good, fallen women becoming chaste, pagans finding Christ – that manner of things.

Have you ever seen it? asked Grimur.

It's locked inside the silver box.

You Christians. You're like women. Always worried about what's in men's hearts. What does an immortal care about one man's heart? Make your sacrifices and observe the law. The rest — love, cures, crops — they're matters for witches.

Martin frowned. *You're wrong, my friend. Jesus is not like other gods. He's not selfish, or quick to anger, and He doesn't ask for sacrifice. He only asks for faith. He died so that we might live. He is the Carpenter of Nazareth. His love for us is as boundless as the sea.*

Martin was quite pleased with that.

Grimur finished his bread. *The sea has boundaries.*

*

Without them noticing, a whole day had passed.

I'm late for Vespers! Martin put down his beer and washed his hands in the cattle trough.

Why did you call him the carpenter of Nazareth?

Because carpentry was His trade. Martin hurried away to the bell tower.

After a few moments the Vespers bell rang out across the island.

Clang! Clang! Clang!

Grimur went back to the refectory wall he had spent the morning plastering. The early evening light caught his work perfectly. The wall was smooth. It would take colour well.

Grimur was pleased.

Thank you, he said to no one in particular.

Chapter 9

Things happen and then they pass.

Atlantic clouds fly over pastures and get caught by the mountains of Mull. Showers follow, soak the bogs and evaporate. Winds stir, sheep gather in the lee of Dùn Ì and then the wind dies again. Sunshine dries the peat.

Saint Fillan, the monastery cat stretches in the sun.

Things happen and then they pass.

*

It was late June, and Blossom was on the wrong side of the island. Without herd boys, the cows of I no longer had guidance as to pasture, and poor Blossom had followed a trail of sweet grass all along the north side of the island until she found herself stuck at the bottom of a sea gulley with the tide slowly coming in.

Now her udder was full, and she was in pain.

From a distance, Una heard the desperate lowing. Finding its source, she slid down slick wet grass onto the beach. She'd brought her pail with her. She tried to milk Blossom to relieve her suffering, but every time she approached, the poor beast backed away.

Blossom wanted Brother Máel Dúin. Every day of her life she'd been tended to by Brother Máel Dúin of the Cows. He had soft grey eyes like the sea in a mist. His voice was gentle. When Máel Dúin placed his hands on Blossom, she felt calm. Where was he? Why wasn't he here? Who was this strange witch?

Come, cow. Come, cow.

Una tried to be commanding, but every time she moved, Blossom dodged her.

Come, cow!

Una made a swift jump, missed and slid into bog.

Damn you, you big hairy shite!

Blossom looked at her.

Moo.

From Dùn Ì, above the gully, Grimur watched.

He was out looking for disturbed earth. He knew Saint Colm's reliquary must be buried somewhere on the hill, so he had decided to search it, inch by inch. Today, however, he'd spent a whole morning walking and seen nothing but puffin tunnels.

Now the cow pushed Una over.

Oh, thank you, my lady. Thank you very much for that kind gesture.

Was she being sarcastic to a cow?

Being tall wasn't helping. Grimur felt a woman needed to be a bit like a cow herself if she wanted to handle them properly. She needed patience and an excess of flesh.

Grimur's half-sister Berta was short and fat, and she had made a fine dairy woman.

The mead wife was all the wrong shape, all the wrong temperament. She was more like a heron, flapping her big ungainly wings.

No wonder the cow kept moving out of reach.

Una was just about in tears when Grimur appeared. He told her to stand aside. Grimur took Blossom's ear and spoke to her in Norse. He used soft words that a cow would understand, the way Berta had shown him when he was a boy. As best he could, he explained to the beast that her usual master was dead. Grimur was going to milk her today. Did she mind? Would she give him permission to begin?

Moo.

Blossom gave permission.

Grimur knelt beside her with the pail. He gripped her fat warm teat at the top and gently squeezed it in his closed fist. Milk squirted into the pail.

Blossom groaned with relief.

Una sat on a rock and watched. He was so gentle with the beast. So careful with the udder. How could these be the same hands that had killed the smith?

Maybe he just really likes tits?

The thought made her laugh out loud. Grimur looked at her, bewildered. She covered her face with her hand. She waved his look away. It was nothing.

Nothing.

*

Later, Martin and Grimur walked together over to the machair with a rope and a collar to bring Blossom home. The low evening sun threw long shadows behind them.

Martin waved midges from his face. *Jesus taught us that every single human being – whoever they may be, whatever their rank or station in life – we all contain a drop of the Holy Spirit.*

Even slaves?

Slaves, women, beggars, children, the sick, the feeble-minded . . . The Holy Spirit is in them all . . . Criminals, sinners, even the lowest of the low. God loves them all. Martin threw up his arms excitably. *Imagine!*

Grimur did imagine. He felt it was an implausible and vaguely comical idea and not one he wanted to spend much time on, because this evening they had to rescue a cow.

It was going to be hard enough work to collar her, never mind to heave her back up the gulley, but, at least, if they could do it soon, then he could bathe his feet in the sea before Vespers, and then he could get back to the cottage, and to Una and her mead.

Martin was still talking. *Every single person on Earth is precious to the Lord!*

I thought you said your god was inconceivable.

He is, but—

I thought you said he was too big to hold in our heads?

That's right!

Then how can he be inside us?

They had crossed to the rocky bays, where the swells were low and quiet. Blossom was calling mournfully from the sand below, the tide at her ankles.

Martin thought, as they scrambled down the grass, then replied: *Every house has a hearth, but we don't understand fire. It's like that. We are each one of us a vessel for the Holy Spirit. Yes!* Martin clapped his hands. *We are each vessels, and the Holy Spirit is liquid. God, when He makes us, pours a drop into each and every one.*

Even Blossom? asked Grimur.

Even Blossom.

God is in a cow, thought Grimur. Is the Holy Spirit milk? Is Jesus the dairy maid? And who drinks the milk? And what about bulls?

As they stumbled down the gulley with their ropes, Grimur came to a conclusion he'd been groping towards from his very first moments on *I*.

Christians are strange.

Blossom regarded the two men with suspicion. Martin looped the collar around her neck. Grimur laid his palm on her warm hairy forehead.

He sang to her an old Norse lullaby:

O hornless cow, rich in milk,
You lick the salty stones all day.
O hornless cow, rich in milk,
The whole world flows from your sweet udder.

While Grimur sang, Martin chanted from Psalm 50:

Every creature of the forest is mine, and the cattle on a
thousand hills.
I know all the birds of the mountains: and the wild beasts
of the field are mine.

Together, their two voices blended and made something
new. Something which seemed to speak to the beast. And
together they led her up the slippery track and back to
safety.

★

Who made *I*? wondered Grimur, as he dipped his hot feet in
the cold clear pool. Which force gathered from the formless
void this spit of sea, granite, bog and sand? And who left it
unfinished, half in and half out of this world? Was it Odin,
flensing the corpse of the giant Ymir? Was it Dana, who
suckled the faeries that shaped the hills of Ireland? Was it
Mamdarrag, the mother serpent whom the Picts honoured?

Or was it this Hebrew god, God, this strange, lonely
spirit to whom Martin gave himself?

Or was *I* here in the beginning? Before all these gods
and spirits? Was the whole world a dream? Still unfinished,
yet to be?

Maybe.

If Grimur had been a prophet, this would have been his
prophesy. But he wasn't, and it isn't, and so these thoughts
are of no more consequence than a lost cow.

*

Grimur washed his body with hot water from the pan.

Una watched him.

Steam rose from his back. The fire smoked gently. Its flame made for a light in which his skin appeared to be the colour of whisky. Water rolled over his shoulders and down the small of his back and dripped onto the flagstone floor.

The scars on his body seemed to her like runes. She felt she could read them.

He pulled his comb through his hair. He oiled his beard. He turned to face her.

Woman! He slapped his chest with his open hand. *Let's drink mead and sing!*

*

Una looked along her shelf of jars. Each jar was marked in a way which only she could understand. Sleep. Sorrel. Anxiety. Intoxication. Singing. Cinnamon. Childbirth. Dancing. Headache. Pain relief. Strawberry. Mint. Menses. Rowan. Plum. Sex.

She chose the one she wanted.

Men were always calling her a witch. She had to be careful. But, she had no spells. She had her mead.

That was power enough.

*

Kneel.

He knelt.

Close your eyes.

He closed his eyes.

Open your mouth.

He opened his mouth.

Drink.

She took a ladle from the jar and poured it into his open mouth.

He swallowed.

Again.

Some spilled around his mouth and beard.

Again.

She drained the last into his open mouth.

He tried to rise.

Wait. Wait.

She stopped him. She untied her tunic. Slipped it from her shoulders. And let it fall to the dirt floor. Dust on her bare feet.

Now you can open your eyes.

He did. He grinned. He grabbed her hips.

★

Finding pleasure in her body was a new experience for Una.

Grimur's desire for her was simple and overwhelming. It was like being covered in honey and going to bed with a bear. Grimur growled at each new part of her. He grinned and laughed and opened his eyes wide in surprise and delight.

The smith was always so unhappy during sex. He would earnestly circumlocute to indicate that he required relief.

She would climb into the cot and pull across the brown curtain. She would lie on the straw, and he would climb on top of her, his face pained and sheepish. This was a different smith to the one who hit her. The man who hit her was a bully. This smith was a pathetic supplicant who desperately wanted the one thing he couldn't have from her: desire. Even had she wished to give it, she had none, not for him at any rate; nor could she feign it, for she did not want to. So, she closed her eyes and turned her head to the side until it was done.

Not now.

Not this night.

Not with a happy bear licking her.

*

Afterwards, Grimur and Una lay together on the straw mattress.

The fire was embers. A thin ribbon of smoke drifted up through the hole in the roof. The cows in the corner radiated damp heat. Grimur smelt the honey sweat on her body. In the firelight and shadow, her face was perfect.

She walked her fingers down his belly.

He looked at her very seriously. She wanted to smile. She also wanted not to. So, she looked very seriously back at him, but she couldn't keep it up. She smiled. She put her hands under the blanket and gripped his warm cock.

Her fingers on his cock felt like safety. He wanted to kiss her. So, he did.

Wouldn't it be good if this never had to end, she thought. But all things do.

I need to piss, he said.

He broke away and trotted across the floor. He opened the door and peed outside. She looked at his bare bum in the moonlight. She wanted to grab it.

Look at him, this barrel of a man, whose bare belly had just lain warm against hers. His eyes were blue as the sea. His face like a mischievous wee boy.

A few weeks ago, she had been lying next to a monster. A few weeks ago, she had assumed, without even realising, that she would go to her grave without ever knowing lust, without ever being touched with love. A few weeks ago, her jokes were kept for the bees. A few weeks ago, she was silent.

Now, this stupid fat Viking shared her bed, and words were flowing between them like two streams meeting in a pool.

It was the loveliest, strangest story she had ever heard, and it was about her.

*

Grimur sat on the bench and stoked the fire. She pulled the blanket around her shoulders and went over to join him in the glow.

Do you have children, Viking?

I don't know.

She frowned. *A man should know if he has children.*

I had two born, he said. *Two girls, Liv and Sif, but I don't know if they're still alive. I left them a dozen years ago. They would be women now, but the last few years were very bad, they say, in Norway. Three harvests failed. Many people died. So, who knows?*

Do you have a wife?

She lives with her brothers in Midsund.

What's her name?

Eir. I think she married again. Helgi told me that once, anyway.

Does that upset you?

Not really.

Because you didn't like her?

No, I liked her very much, but we weren't a good match.

Why not?

Her father wanted to kill me.

Oh.

That's why I left.

What's she like?

Small. Funny. She rides horses well.

You like funny women.

He blushed. He'd never thought of it. *I like other things in a woman too.*

Like what?

Like cooking and mead-making and . . .

What?

Poor animal husbandry.

Shh.

I'm teasing you.

She curled into his body. A light wind sang in the eaves.

Why was she here? he thought. This heron-shaped woman, hiding in this Christian hovel? This woman was as grand and magnificent as Freya or Gerth. Why wasn't she holding court in the middle of some mead hall – a tall elm, hanging with beautiful jewellery?

Instead, here she was, sitting with a fat old Viking, naked but for a horsehair blanket, her grey-blonde hair tied up with a red woollen band.

*

He touched her face. *What happened to your cheek?*

The smith broke my jaw with a poker.

Why did he do that?

I told him a joke.

You told him a joke, and he broke your jaw?

Yes.

Was the joke that bad?

No, it was a good joke.

Tell me.

She hesitated. No one in the world knew this. *I had done something which annoyed him. I can't remember what. He admonished me as if I were a child. I said it didn't matter. The smith said it did matter because God sees everything. I said this thing was a thing too little for even God to care about. The smith said: 'Wife, it's my duty to correct you. I am your husband, and I am telling you now, God cares very, very, very much about even the smallest things.'*

And I said: 'Well, it's good to know he cares about your dick then.'

Grimur snorted a big horse laugh. *You didn't?*

I did.

He imagined the smith's face. He laughed again.

What's funny? she asked.

You, he said.

He broke my jaw!

That made him laugh even more. She'd known it would.

Grimur sputtered mead into the fire. Tears came to his eyes.

Now she, too, was laughing. His laughter fanned hers, and hers his. They fell off the bench, and their entangled gasping, giggles, guffaws and squeaks drifted up through the hole in the roof and joined the slowly winding smoke as it rose into the star-spattered night.

Martin heard them. He wrapped himself tightly in his blanket. The laughter made him smile.

Maybe, when it reached Heaven, it would make God smile, too.

Who knows?

Chapter 10

As June bled into July, Una worked to keep them fed.
She made porridge. She butchered sheep. She gathered
seaweed. She made bread, and she prepared the skins of
seals to make a cover for the straw mattress.

Grimur fixed up the cottage. It hadn't been well taken
care of. The smith had always preferred metal to wood.
He spent his time working on gates and hinges, door keys
and horseshoes. The smith thought wood was for peasants.
The cottage belonged to his wife. As long as he was fed,
warmed and unchallenged, the smith really didn't care
what his house looked like.

Grimur thought if you were lucky enough to have a
cottage, you should look after it. Grimur had never had a
cottage.

He repaired the walls with mud and lime. He tidied up
the roof thatch, fixed the benches and strengthened the
bed.

*

Martin worked in the scriptorium.

The last chapters of the *Gospel of John the Apostle* are dark and hard. They mostly tell of betrayal, trial, scourging and crucifixion. Every line is soaked in pain and loss. Martin didn't have the skill yet to find comfort in this brutal story of execution and shame.

The sorrow was heavy.

Aed had taught Martin there were three different ways to understand scripture.

1. The Present Meaning
2. The Hidden Meaning
3. The Mysteries

*

1.

The present meaning was the easiest. This was the struggle to understand what the sentence appeared to mean on its surface. To produce this meaning, one had to understand Latin and Greek. You had to know how particular words were used then and now. You had to place those words in context. You had to stand back and see how a sentence fitted into its verses, its chapter and its book.

2.

The second layer of meaning was hidden. To obtain this meaning, the monk had to decode secret patterns. These were patterns born of complex analogy. Things also meant other things. In this layer, one might find, for example, that in John 4, when Christ talks with the Samaritan woman at the well, the hidden meaning is that the widow is us, Samaria the fallen world, and the water in the well is God.

3.

Finally, the monk must approach the mysteries which lie behind the scriptures.

Since God was beyond understanding, God's words must also be beyond understanding. All human readings of scripture were, by definition, degraded, earthly and failed. The moment a monk felt that he had understood a line, he must, at the same time, realise he had not.

It was frustrating.

However, if the monk were able to truly accept this impossibility, yet still give himself wholly and completely to the text, then perhaps, by the grace of God, he would be granted a brief glimpse of the mysteries behind the words.

Christ's hand would draw back the curtain of the world for a moment, and the monk would be allowed to briefly bathe in the blinding, overwhelming, flooding light of God's truth before the curtain closed again and all was gone.

Such glimpses were, by definition, impossible to capture in words.

Had Aed had such a moment? Martin once asked him.

No, said Aed. *Not yet.*

Chapter 11

Grimur's dreams were troubled that summer. He was visited by his mother, his half-sister, his daughters (who it turned out were alive) and his father, who came to him singing the songs of his boyhood.

Sometimes the visits were blessings, sometimes goodbyes.

Grimur didn't discuss his dreams with Una. She had no interest. She told him dreams were nothing more than overheard conversations from a world behind this world. Not meant for us.

One night, Eir came to Grimur in the form of a seal. She lay on a rock and spoke to him tenderly . . . *You will be changed,* she said. As she spoke, she lay a warm wet flipper on his face. Her eyes were black and wet. She opened her fish-smelling mouth to kiss him. He woke with a start.

*

The next morning, Grimur knelt down in the middle of the scriptorium.

Cloud-softened sunlight filled the room. The air sparkled with dust.

Martin sat on a wooden stool beside him.

Begin.

Grimur closed his eyes.

I was born on a jarl's farm in Ålesund. The jarl was called Fat Eye. My mother was his wife. My father was a slave from Ireland and a carpenter. He made things for the farm. Fat Eye spent ten years in the East, trading on the rivers. When he came back to Ålesund, he killed my father and adopted me. Fat Eye taught me to fight.

I was given to be married to a girl on the next estate. Her father didn't like me, so I burned down his cowshed. I could have loved my wife, but I didn't want to be murdered, so I went with the first jarl who came looking for Vikings. That man was Ásleif Cracked-Tooth. He was a good captain. When he was killed, I sailed with his nephew Helgi Cleanshirt, who built a hall in Shetland.

The first innocent I killed was at the age of twelve. Fat Eye told me to behead the old ploughman, who had become feeble-minded. He didn't want to feed him any more. I raised an axe over the old man's head. He shivered with fear. Fat Eye said to bring the blade down as hard as I could. I did. Two hands. Full force. The old man's head rolled clear in the mud. His red eyes looked up at me. Fat Eye said: 'Well done, boy.'

I didn't kill anyone innocent again until I was twenty-five, when Ásleif took the fort of Mousa and there was a general slaughter. We killed everyone. Once we defeated the warriors, we killed the peasants. I stabbed four men. I cut the throat of an old woman. I pushed a wife under the wheels of an ox cart. I never killed any children. Not for any reason, really. Mostly just sentiment. Where women and children were concerned, I preferred to take slaves.

We went into battle many times. We battled Eric Dog Nose, and the Saxons of Yarmouth, and the Egil of Jutland, and the Picts of Orkney, and the Picts of Tain, and the Picts of Thurso, and there was a trip to Ireland, and we also sailed once to Aldeigjuborg in the East, but we mostly traded there and didn't do any fighting. After Ásleif died, Helgi was my jarl.

During those adventures I should think I must have killed a few dozen innocent people.

Martin nodded, slightly stunned. *How many, exactly?*

Grimur used his fingers to help him count. *Thirty-two?*

So, you have murdered a total of thirty-eight innocent people?

Wait, forty.

Forty?

Oh, and the smith of I.

Forty-one?

Why don't we say fifty, to be safe?

Martin considered. *Brother Grimur, do you truly repent of your sins?*

I do, Grimur said.

Will you obey the Law of the Innocents henceforward, and only kill men in battle?

I will.

Martin put his hand on the Northman's head. *You are forgiven.*

Martin told Grimur that, in penance, he should work

for the monastery for fifty whole weeks, which would be one week for every soul he had taken.

And that was that.

His slate was clean.

★

Now it was high summer. Night made hardly a smear on the long blue days. The island had long forgotten the ache of winter's grip. Bees hovered over the flowers in the garden even into the late evening. Small birds shouted to each other in the oak grove.

Grimur stood on the abbot's rock and looked out to sea.

His flesh turned to wood.

He became a tree . . .

His roots reached down into *I*, curling and splitting like the inside of a lung. His arms became branches, reaching up and multiplying, his hands sprouting thin green leaves and clouds of pale blossom.

. . . an ash.

The bell rang Compline.

Clang! Clang! Clang!

Chapter 12

Men! You men!

Grimur and Martin turned to see who was calling.

It was a young woman.

God's blessings to you!

She carefully navigated the muddy path through the broken monastery gates. She was a slight woman, with waist-length red hair and freckled milky skin. Her embroidered cape was long and blue, and, on her feet, she wore soft leather boots.

I'm looking for Abbot Blathmac. She was Irish, from the North. *Would you know where he is?*

Grimur didn't want to answer.

Martin spoke shyly. *My lady, he's with his Lord.*

In Kilmartin?

In Heaven.

She stared at them, bewildered. *But I've come all the way from Antrim.* She sat down on the church step.

Grimur and Martin looked at each other. Neither could make any sense of this.

Finally, she spoke, exasperated. *Last month, Abbot Blathmac came to me in a dream. He said I should come immediately because I was called by Christ to be an anchoress. He told me if I proved my faith in Christ and left my life behind me, he would provide me with a cell and books and guidance.*

Grimur noticed her pale hands balling into pink fists. *I'm sorry your journey has been wasted.*

Martin tried to explain. *The Northmen came in spring. They put our brothers to the sword and set fire to all the buildings. Then they murdered our beloved Father Abbot Blathmac by tearing him apart with horses. After that, the island was cleared. The mead wife and us are the only souls left.*

The woman took a moment to absorb this new information. *Well, one of you must be the abbot now . . . Which one of you is it?*

Grimur pointed to Martin.

Before he could protest, the woman knelt at Martin's feet. *Father Abbot, accept me.*

She took his hand and kissed it. This sparrow, this skelf, thought Grimur, would consume Martin like a worm.

I beg of you.

Martin looked at Grimur for help. The Northman shrugged. Personally, he couldn't think of a greater waste of life than a girl like this giving her life in service to the weird god, God. Why couldn't she just throw herself on a pyre like any normal woman? But what did he know? He'd only been Christian for a couple of days.

Sister, we accept you, said Martin, in the most abbot-like voice he could muster.

Thank you, she said, rising briskly from her knees. *I will need a bed, a desk, some ink, some vellum and a chanty.*

Martin hesitated.

Now, please bring me some food and a cell into which I can be bricked.

Grimur rescued him. *Father Abbot, would you like me to undertake these arrangements?*

Martin nodded. *God bless you, both.*

Satisfied, the woman brushed the dust off her cloak, bade them good day, strode into the church, bowed before the broken altar and offered a long and grateful prayer of thanks to Saint Colm.

*

She ate soup. It was only mutton stock and barley, but it was welcome after two days on an open boat.

Brother Martin sat opposite her. When she was finished, he spoke. *What's your name?*

Bronagh.

And what brings you to I?

I am a humble woman from Ireland who wants to give herself to God.

Sister Bronagh, tell me the truth.

That was interesting.

Brother Martin laid his hands flat on the refectory table and tried to keep his voice steady.

Sister Bronagh, your cloak is plaid, your hair is held in a silver clasp, your feet are shod with boots of calf leather and you give orders to men. You may be from Ireland, you may be a woman, but, whatever you are, you are not humble.

She narrowed her eyes. *You have a good eye for clothes, Brother Martin, but you can't see into a person's heart. If you could, you would see that I am, in fact, a very humble woman, certainly humbler than most women who come to this church – perhaps even the humblest.*

She felt herself rise on the swell of her own argument.

You might think only a poor woman can be humble, but, if such a woman gives her life to the Church, she doesn't have to give up very much since she doesn't have very much to start with. I, on the other hand, who was blessed with servants, comfort, honour and jewels, have given away everything. I don't think it's possible to be more humble than that.

She wondered if she ought to write this down. These were the sorts of insight she could probably expect quite often now that she was an anchoress.

Brother Martin was not persuaded. *Sister, who are your people?*

She saw she could hide no longer. The monk had a young face but, clearly, he had a sharp mind. She would have to confess.

My name is Bronagh mac Eochada . . .

He left space for her to continue.

. . . youngest daughter of Eoin mac Eochada, prince of the

Dál Fiatach, brother of Muiredach mac Eochada, High King of Ulaid.

Does your father know you are here?

No.

And what brings you to I, Bronagh mac Eochada?

It's this or be married. She looked away, ashamed.

Martin softened. *Welcome to I, Sister Bronagh.*

★

Bronagh followed Martin into the church, dipping her knee as she entered.

He led her to the altar. Together they knelt before Christ and crossed themselves. Martin felt quite proud to show Jesus his new friend, and Bronagh was hungry for the new. She'd spent far too long with women in the dark back rooms of Dún Pádraig castle. Her eyes were wide now, for new pictures, new colours, new faces and new feelings.

What possessions have you?

A purse full of silver to pay for my keep, my clothes, my embroidery and a book.

Bronagh reached into her cloth bag and brought out a waxed cloth parcel. *It was made for me by the monks of Nendrum, as a gift from my father.*

Martin unfolded the package carefully. He gasped. Inside was a small, perfect, beautiful copy of the *Song of Songs*.

You prepared well.

Thank you.

She gave her things to him. He laid them out on the wooden pew between them. Then, he asked her to kneel on a sealskin pad and he began her instruction in the Rules of Colm Cille.

First, said Martin, *you must be alone.*

This would be no struggle. She was always alone.

Be naked always, in imitation of Christ.

Her eyes widened until Martin explained.

This means you must own nothing. No possessions, no jewellery, no objects or disguises which stand between you and the Lord. You must be as simple as Christ when He entered Jerusalem.

Fine. Simple is good.

Everything must be shared.

I have nothing now anyway.

Lock yourself away, with only one door.

Taken as read.

Listen to religious men.

This made her smile. She interrupted brightly. *Like you?*

Martin couldn't tell if she was teasing or being sincere. He paused.

She winked at him.

Winked?!

Martin continued, blushing. *Don't listen to fools but instead bless them.*

Part one: easy. Part two: a struggle.

Be discreet.

Who, me?

Submit to every rule of devotion. Prepare your mind for martyrdom. Prepare your mind for persecution. Forgive everyone. Pray for those who trouble you. Sing the Office of the Dead for every soul as if it were for your dearest friend . . .

Hours passed as he talked. Wind and cold rain blustered outside. The candles guttered, and she noticed their bodies dance on the shadowed wall.

Stand to sing hymns. Keep constant vigil. Pray, work and read. Work always. Keep everything in its proper order.

Swallows sang in the roof beams, the sun fell into the sea and Blossom lowed in the yard.

Bronagh felt she was a soldier being armoured for the fray. Martin felt he was her armourer.

Always give alms. Don't eat unless you're hungry. Don't sleep unless you're tired. Don't speak unless you have to. Everything you get, give it away. Love God with all your heart and strength. Love your neighbour as yourself and obey the testaments of God at all times.

Surely that one's obvious? She was growing bored of this now.

Complacency is the mother of sin, Martin countered sternly.

A look passed between them. He wondered if she might strike him. She didn't.

Of course, Father, she said, primly.

There is only one more rule, and Abbot Blathmac always said it was the most important rule of all.

What is it, Father?

Pray . . . Pray until you cry. Read until you cry. Give yourself up to all God's tasks until you cry, and, if you can't cry, sweat.

The rain passed, the wind was slack, and seagulls scratched at the late afternoon air with their calls.

Bronagh rose. *Show me to my cell.*

*

Una pulled open the rough wooden door.

The room had been a grain store. It was eight paces wide by six paces long and about the height of a horse. The roof was timber and thatch.

It smelt of cold stone, barley and earth.

Bronagh could just make out a chair, a chamber pot, a writing table and some parchment. On the table was her pocket copy of the *Song of Songs*.

The only light came from a high hatch through which grain had previously been poured. It made a rectangle of pale sky against the dark brown wall.

This is the room in which I will spend the rest of my life, she thought. Confined in body, yes, but free to roam the infinite expanse of the divine. Finally, she was to be an anchoress.

Grimur will cut a hatch in the door, here, said Una. *You can pull it aside when you want to speak to people. There's a small bell on the table to ring if you need anything. There's a hole in the wall over there where you can put out your pot in the morning. I'll leave food twice a day, as I do for Brother Martin. Is there anything else you need?*

No, said Bronagh, perhaps a little too firmly.

Fear hung in the air for a moment. Bronagh was unsure which one of them it belonged to.

Eventually Una spoke. *My lady, you're young, and, God willing, you have many years ahead of you. When you're young, the weight of the future can seem a burden at times, but I want to tell you, in each day which passes, no matter how hard it feels to bear, you can find something, something to lighten the load: a joke, a face, some food, a song, a child, a man. Sometimes all of them in one day.*

Bronagh realised she was being scolded.

But, my lady, all those comforts are out there. In here . . . in here there's nothing.

Bronagh flicked the table. *There's God.*

Maybe.

Are you a theologian?

No.

Well, then.

Una bowed her head slightly. *God's blessings to you. If you need anything, ring, and I'll come.*

She shut the door behind her.

Bronagh heard the door lock.

The cell was dark.

Chapter 13

It was August, and it was hot.

Bronagh knelt on the dirt floor of the cell and traced her finger over the page.

My beloved is to me like a pouch of myrrh, which lies all night between my breasts.

My beloved is to me like a cluster of henna flowers in the vineyards of En Gedi.

What did it mean?

What was myrrh? Did it grow on vines? What was henna? Where was En Gedi?

And what did any of it have to do with breasts?

She read it again.

And again.

And again.

A bead of sweat ran down her forehead, on to her cheek, then dropped onto her chest.

Outside, she heard the boy sing Terce in the yard.

She rang the handbell.

Ting! Ting! Ting!

*

Martin knelt at the hatch and listened as she recited the verse.

My beloved is to me like a pouch of myrrh, which lies all night between my breasts.

My beloved is to me like a cluster of henna flowers in the vineyards of En Gedi.

In her voice, the words seemed richer than he'd known them before. Heady and strange. He'd only ever heard them spoken by Brother Aed before, but in Bronagh's accent, in the precise curving sounds of the North, she seemed to bend the words anew.

Bronagh knelt in the dark on the other side of the door.

What does it mean?

The wind blew through the trees on the other side of the yard. It left little devils of dung dust spinning in its wake.

Brother Martin, are you there?

I am here, Sister Bronagh.

She tried again. *What does it mean?*

It speaks of Christ.

Chapter 14

I was hot.

In the oak grove, finches tumbled and whirled, wheeling like sycamore seeds till they dropped onto the abbot's grave and mated.

Bees hovered around white valerian, climbing into flowers, sucking at nectar.

Grimur scythed in the hay meadow.

Una sat on a stool, pulled her skirt up over her knees, took off her boots and let her bare feet rest on the cool grass.

Watching Grimur work.

*

My beloved is to me as a pouch of myrrh, which lies all night between my breasts.

My beloved is to me as a cluster of henna flowers in the vineyards of En Gedi.

Bronagh read it again.

And again.

And again.

A bead of sweat ran down her forehead, onto her cheek, and dropped onto her chest.

In the distance she heard Martin chant Prime.

She rang her handbell.

Ting! Ting! Ting!

*

A warm wind blew through the yard, leaving little devils of dung dust spinning in its wake.

Martin offered a reading from memory.

Myrrh is a perfume which smells like pine on a warm evening. Henna is a flower which grows among rocks and has the fragrance of roses. En Gedi is the name of a spring in the desert.

This verse tells us that the king and his lover are lying together on his couch. His head lies on her breast, and she breathes in his spirit as if it were myrrh. She tells us that he is, to her, as perfect, as rare, as lovely, as a flower in a desert.

That's what I thought it meant. Thank you. Bronagh made to shut the hatch.

Of course, that's just the surface meaning. To properly understand the text, you have to look for the hidden meaning.

Please tell.

In this text, the king stands for Christ and the lover stands for us. When we are good, when we obey God's holy law, then Christ loves us. He brings Himself closer to us, and allows us to hold Him, to feel Him, to sense Him, to revel in His perfection.

Silence.

Martin wasn't sure if Bronagh was still there.

Normally, we can't experience God without being overwhelmed. So, God sent us perfection in the form of a man. When we experience Jesus as vulnerable and alone, like a flower in the desert, then we, His lovers, are given the gift of His scent, His presence, His holiness pouring into our souls.

Silence.

Martin lowered his gaze. She mouthed the verses. He watched her lips.

Eventually she spoke. *Is there a third meaning?*

There is, but we won't get into that today.

God bless you, Brother Martin.

God bless you, Sister Bronagh.

She shut the hatch.

★

August passed in squalls and fitful breezes.

Without really noticing, they settled into a rhythm of the days. At dawn, Una made porridge. After she and Grimur had eaten, they brought bowls to Sister Bronagh and Brother Martin.

Una slid Bronagh's food through the low hatch, then reached in to remove the chanty pot, which she emptied and returned.

Grimur spent the day with the livestock, or repairing and securing the monastery buildings, while Una cooked a broth, baked the day's bread, attended the bees, brewed beer and, finally, in the late afternoon, wandered the island to gather seaweed, herbs, flowers, roots, berries, leaves, bones, blood, milk, stones, waters and all the many other ingredients which contributed to her beer.

Martin wrote.

Bronagh went mad with boredom and loneliness. Sometimes she read. Sometimes she invented songs. Sometimes she hallucinated. Sometimes she lay down on the bed and gave herself to Jesus.

As daylight ebbed, Una would feed them all with barley broth, bread and a flask of mead.

In the evening, Martin sang the offices and prayed. Bronagh stared at her square of sky and waited for sleep. Grimur and Una sat by the fire and told jokes until nightfall.

This was how the days passed.

Until they changed.

Chapter 15

Several horsemen had gathered on the beach at Fionnphort. A boat stood ready to cross the sound. On a black pony, in their midst, sat a portly, grey-haired man in robes.

Are they coming over here? Grimur was anxious. *They'll know I'm Norse.*

Not if you're quiet, said Una.

How can I be quiet? They'll ask who I am. They'll ask what I'm doing here. Then what will I say?

Just say you're a monk!

Una found an old cassock in the dormitory store. Grimur pulled it over his head and tied it up at the waist. Then he knelt by the cattle trough. Martin stood behind him with cold water and a knife. He shaved a rough tonsure into Grimur's scalp. The Viking watched his beautiful hair drop in gorgeous clumps down into the black water. His reflection looked surprisingly Christian.

Later, he slid the knife into his britches.

Not that Christian.

*

Domhnall of Crinan led Bishop Fiachra around the monastery grounds. Domhnall was impressed by the extent of the repair work since the massacre. The boy monk and his hairy convert had clearly worked hard. The bishop, however, could only see ruin.

Bishop Fiachra of Kilmartin felt his task, in relation to God, was similar to that of a provincial official deputising for an emperor. That is to say, he saw it as largely confined to accurate accounting and the production of an annual report. Although the monastery was technically within the bishopric of Argyll, it had been independent for many years. During all that time, Bishop Fiachra had neither had to account for nor report on it. Now, however, just when it had become an unproductive, trouble-hungry wreck, it was on his books.

Thanks, Vikings.

The bishop would happily have abandoned *I* years ago. It was in a terrible location, out on the sea roads, far from the king's men. Frankly, it was always a massacre waiting to happen, and he'd seen it coming years ago. Blathmac's obsessive zealotry had put good churchmen's necks under the pagan sword. And peasants. It was ridiculous, upsetting, unnecessary – embarrassing, even.

He addressed the boy monk. *Every time they come, the damage gets worse.*

We're making progress, Your Excellency, with the help of God. For example, Brother Grimur has repaired the scriptorium. Martin pointed to a patch of new thatch. *We've begun work on the church roof, repaired the barns and grain stores, secured the cattle pastures and planted new barley. It's a lot.*

The bishop stared at the sea. It was particularly blue today.

Domhnall tried to help the boy. *Perhaps, Your Excellency, if God wills it and the Church can spare the coins, I could arrange a work party of men from Mull to come over and help the brothers with reconstruction?*

No. The bishop was adamant. *The Church has no money.*

Domhnall shrugged. The bishop's rings alone could purchase an entire estate.

Besides, the Northmen will come back. They always do. They're wolves. Anything we build is just bait. We should abandon it all.

Grimur noticed a line of crows watching them from an old oak.

I *is a holy place.* Martin's voice quavered.

It is, Brother Martin, a holy place — a holy place made sacred by the blood of martyrs, and we don't want any more of that, do we? We don't want to throw even more souls to the pagans.

The crows took flight, like dark thoughts.

Jesus said that, when struck, we must turn the other cheek, Martin tried.

That doesn't mean what you think it means. There was an edge of irritation to the bishop's voice.

What does it mean?

It means that if someone strikes us, we should turn our cheek, like this − the bishop used his finger to physically turn Martin's cheek − *and walk away. We must not succumb to the vanity of resistance. Instead, we should accept the humility of self-preservation. We are children of God. In this text, Jesus asks that we take care of ourselves, so we can give more of our glory to Him.*

This was a novel exegesis to which Martin had no answer.

*

Bishop Fiachra and Domhnall ate thick lamb stew and drank warm mead in the cottage. They were silent. Una had fed them well. Perhaps the meal had softened them because after a while the bishop put his hand on Martin's shoulder and spoke to him kindly.

Son, I'll let you stay in this hopeless place on one condition: that you collect twelve jars of this woman's mead and give it over to the bishopric every year in rent.

Thank you, Your Excellency.

My stewards will come in November.

With that, Bishop Fiachra rose, discreetly farted and gave Una a small silver coin.

Father, before you go . . .

The bishop's face fell. Jesus Christ, the faithful were a pain in the hole.

Will you hear my sins and give me penance?

*

Martin knelt by the cross of Saint John. Fiachra sat on a milking stool.

A kestrel hunted in the new-mown meadow.

Father . . . Martin took a deep breath. This was going to be hard. *I have taken the Lord's name in vain, at least eight times, maybe more, particularly when I've felt despair or grief, or in the long nights when—*

Just stick to the sins, son. There's a boat waiting.

Bishop Fiachra shifted on the stool and wondered if he shouldn't take a jar of mead with him today.

Chastened, Martin summarised his misdemeanours. *I have . . . I have . . . I have . . .*

Each confession felt a bit like vomit, a purging, a slurry of failure heaved up from his heart. And, like being sick, just when you thought it was done, there was always more to come up.

I have . . . I have . . . I have . . .

Until, finally, Martin fell, wrung out, empty and exhausted, on the grass at the bishop's feet.

For these and all my sins I am truly sorry.

The kestrel dived, silent, talons out.

Father?

Hmm?

For these and all my sins I am truly sorry.

The bishop blinked, shook his head and slapped himself. *Very good, son. You're a good lad. God bless you. No penance required.*

And that was that.

His slate was clean.

Bishop Fiachra and Domhnall left on the turning tide, each holding a jar of mead.

Martin felt God's mercy wash across the shoaling beach of his soul.

The kestrel ate the field mouse.

Chapter 16

By September the surviving lambs were strong. Even an eagle wouldn't try for those big lads.

Yellow yorlins and purple finches fought in clouds around the apple trees.

In scraggy rigs the barley browned.

★

Martin tried to work.

No woman is more consuming of a man's imagination than one who is locked away. The less there is to see, the more there is to imagine. Martin was aware of this weakness and so, to keep temptation at bay, he spent his evenings meditating on the rotting corpses of the saints: worms sucking the deliquesced eyeballs of Saint Augustine, stinking flesh falling from the green bones of Saint Bridget, the black brain soup of Saint Cuthbert bubbling with porcelain maggots.

Nevertheless, he found himself hovering by the door to Bronagh's cell.

Daily.

There was usually a reason: to bring a book, to offer food, to comment on the weather. But sometimes he just stood, holding his breath, trying to feel her presence on the other side of the door.

*

One morning, in early September, the cell was silent.

Was she sleeping? Was she gone? It was still warm. The tide was out. The island was fat and sleepy, heavy with ripening crops. Martin leaned in close to the door, not touching, as if the wood was her skin, as if touching it would waken her.

The hatch opened.

Brother Martin?

Sister Bronagh!

The dark rectangle framed her mouth perfectly: pale skin, a hint of freckles, pink lips.

What do you want?

Worms. Eyeballs. Maggots. Flesh. Worms. Eyeballs. Maggots. Flesh.

Oh . . . em . . . I . . .

How long had she been sitting there?

. . . I wondered how you were after the rain last night?

Was there rain last night?

There was, around Matins.

I was asleep.

Good.

Martin knelt, cassock in the mud, so his face could be

closer to hers. Puddle water seeped through his robes and
wet his legs.

*Sister Bronagh, I wondered if you might help me with some
scripture?*

Of course, Brother Martin.

From this angle he could see the top of her cheek, a
glimpse of her left eye.

I'm working on chapter nineteen of the Gospel of John *and
there's a passage I still don't understand.*

I see.

May I share the words with you?

Please.

Bronagh sat on the low stool and watched his mouth as
he spoke. His chin was dotted with barley-stubble hair. She
couldn't see his eyes, but she could imagine them.

'*The soldiers came, and they broke the limbs of the first
criminal, and of the other who had been crucified with him. When
they came to Jesus, and when they saw that he was already dead,
they did not break his limbs. But one of the soldiers pierced his side
with a spear, and immediately blood and water came forth.'*

She felt the heat of the sun on one cheek and the cold
of the shade on the other. *Where are you lost, Brother Martin?*

I'm lost in the water and the blood.

Daylight from the high window cut a bright shaft
diagonally across the room. About a third of the way down
it was crossed by light coming from the door hatch.

A dead body doesn't bleed, and a dead body has no water in it. *So why does blood and water come forth from the body of the Lord?*

Repeat the text, please.

Martin did as she asked.

Bronagh considered the words. She saw the cross of light and opened her heart to the Holy Spirit.

After a while, she spoke. *There are three keys to the scripture, Brother Martin. Blood is faith. Water is truth. The Crucifixion brought forth a river of faith and a river of truth. Like blood and water. If we meditate on the Crucifixion, we, too, will be flooded with faith and truth.*

I see.

But the text also calls to mind the blood and water of birth. When a woman gives birth, the baby comes out in a rush of blood and water. It tells us that, at his moment of death, Christ birthed a new world. Like a baby, this new world was wholly innocent, full of love and completely in need of our protection.

Martin saw that she was right. *Thank you, Sister Bronagh.*

You're welcome, Brother Martin.

She closed the hatch.

Chapter 17

It rained.

For a few days and nights, heavy clouds hung over the island and dropped seasons of water in hours. A succession of warm windless showers made the burns run lively. Puddles formed on the church floor. A new loch was created in the bottom pasture, which became a home for wild duck.

Unable to work, Grimur decided to go to church and listen to Martin's offices.

Hearing him chant hymns, recite the strange poetry of scripture and reflect on God, the master maker — *who shaped and carved every leaf on every tree, every hair on every head, every drop of rain, every tear, every seed, every beast, every heart* — Grimur wondered if he, too, might experience that thing which Martin had called 'faith'.

So, he tried.

He gave himself completely to the sermons. He opened himself to the songs. He felt himself tremble on the edge of revelation all through the long, rain-softened days.

But nothing.

He could sense the possibility of faith. But it was on the other side of a wall. A wall in which he could see no door.

The rain stopped.

Grimur left the church and stood by the great stone cross of Saint John.

At that moment, a rainbow formed, making an arch from mainland to island.

But that's when rainbows form, isn't it?

When the sun shines after a storm.

It doesn't mean anything.

★

By September's middle, two months had passed since Bronagh anchored herself on *I*, but she had long ago lost track of time. Hours felt like days; weeks sped by in hours. She hardly ate. She bled all the time or she didn't bleed at all.

Day merged with night.

She prayed. She slept. She watched sunlight cross the floor of her cell. She sat on the chair. She read *Song of Songs*. She ate bread and soup. She prayed again. She slept. She sang old songs.

She imagined Jesus.

She imagined Jesus's hair. She imagined touching it. Smelling it. She imagined His cheek. Stroking it. She imagined His chest, the shape of it, the strange colour of His skin, the heat of His human body. She imagined His arms. Carpenter's arms.

Jesus held His open palms to her. She saw His wounds. He smiled at her. She imagined His face. He touched her breast. His touch conveyed total love. Everything that was bad about her, He knew and forgave. Everything good about her, He saw and magnified. Her oddness, to Him, was beautiful. Her strange heart, He understood.

★

In the church, at the same time, Martin knelt on the cold stone floor in front of the altar and tried to see behind the curtain of the world. It was so hard to do it alone. He'd observed the rules and prayed. He'd meditated with all his soul. He had kept the flame of Christ alive. He had honoured the bones of Colmcille. But still he had not seen beyond.

Maybe if he tried harder than he had ever tried before? Maybe if he gave himself over completely to the point of exhaustion? Maybe then he would glimpse God?

Maybe.

Of course, in one sense, Martin saw God every day, but those were just ordinary noticings: geese crossing the sky, a duck landing on water, the music of the sea, the arrival of plums on a branch – all beautiful, but, in the end, merely decorative.

Nor did Martin give much value to those common moments when he felt his soul opening, raw, tangible and physical – like in the afterglow of a grief, or remembering his mother, or following a kindness.

Those moments were like seeing the house of God from the outside.

Martin wanted to enter the house. He wanted to be surrounded by God, to be one with God, to dissolve in the enormity of God, to swim in the everything and always of God, to find his soul in the unimaginable and universal NOW of God.

That's what Martin wanted.

But tonight, on the cold stone floor, God felt further away than ever. The rough cloth of his cassock rubbed on his bare buttocks as he tossed and turned.

Tonight, all he could think of was Sister Bronagh.

Worms. Eyeballs. Maggots. Flesh. Worms. Eyeballs. Maggots. Flesh.

Worms. Eyeballs. Maggots. Flesh. Worms. Eyeballs. Maggots. Flesh.

Sister Bronagh.

Sister Bronagh.

Sister Bronagh . . .

With a furious grunt of failure, Martin gave up the vanity of resistance and, instead, fell to imagining Sister Bronagh with all the detail and clarity as if he were diving into a pool of sin. Her hair was a scarlet halo. Her pale blue eyes, the gates of chaos. He imagined her on her knees, in flowered grass by the orchard wall, her long fingers steepled, her blue robe tight across her shoulders, praying to the Lord like an illuminated illustration of Mary Magdalene herself.

Sister Bronagh.

Sister Bronagh.

Sister Bronaaaagh . . .

Martin had sinned.

★

In her cell, Bronagh lay on her bed naked and watched the moonlight cross the floor.

Jesus' head lay on her breast. White flowers in His hair. She inhaled the heady scent of grace.

And she was – finally and completely – whole.

★

In the cottage, beasts stirred. Grimur snored. Una wondered if her bees were safe.

The wind blew.

★

The next morning, Bronagh's cell was empty.

The *Song of Songs* lay open on her table.

On the first page was a note written in splattery ink and a wobbly hand.

Faith is not enough.

Chapter 18

In August, the puffins had left *I*. A thousand tiny bird ships with multi-coloured head-prows bob on the wild green sea.

Now, the island begins to fall quiet.

*

Grimur sat on top of Dùn Ì and looked west across the big whale roads. Below him he saw Una feeding her hives. A melancholy song of Nones drifted from the church.

Martin sang less now Bronagh had gone. She had crawled through the food hatch, flagged a passing boat to Fionnphort and, according to news from Una's relatives shouted from the other side of the sound, paid some fishermen to take her back to Ireland.

The seals on the north beaches made a sad harmony with Martin's lament. Gulls rose and fell on the warm winds.

Unlike Martin, Grimur felt content. Why shouldn't he? He was fed and fucked and far away from trouble. Perhaps this was what Christians meant by Heaven: a simple sufficiency? If Grimur had died in battle, he'd go to the great hall of Odin where he'd be expected to fight every day and drink with pricks for all eternity.

I was better.

He worked, he repaired, he ate and, at night, he fell into a bed with a warm bosomy woman.

Yes, this was Heaven.

And that was when Grimur saw it.

On the very stone on which he was sitting – between his legs, almost pointing at his crotch . . .

A cross.

Someone had pecked it out of the rock with a stone or a hammer. Whoever it was, they were no craftsman. The marking was faint, and without the long shadow, he'd never have seen it at all; but tracing his fingers across the stone, he could feel it clearly.

Grimur had an idea who had made this cross in the rock and an idea why.

The stone was about the size of a dog. He squatted down and grabbed it in his arms. He pulled with all his force. The boulder shifted and gave. It had been loosened before.

Grimur rolled it over and saw a glint in the brown wormy earth underneath.

A silver box.

It was about the size of a woman's jewellery case. The silver was elaborately decorated with spirals, circles and curls. He put it down on the grass and lay down prostrate in front of it. It wasn't that he wanted to show obeisance:

he wanted to open the lid, and he wasn't sure what spirits might come out.

Grimur pinched his fingers on the little handle and opened the lid.

It gave a little metallic squeak.

Nothing.

Grimur peered inside.

The box was empty but for a small red velvet cushion. The cushion had a long dark stain along its middle. A discolouration. The whole gave off the distant smell of incense.

That was it.

If there had ever been a finger here, it had long ago crumbled to dust. All that was left was a ghost in the form of a long dark stain on the velvet cushion.

Grimur closed the box.

*

We could go to Constantinople?

He'd come into the brewhouse. Una was making up batches in quantity now. It was a busy time. Outside, a squall had blown in. Grimur's hair was wet. The wind stirred the thatch.

I thought . . . you and me . . .

She took her knife to some seaweed and chopped it increasingly fine.

Summer will end.

Did he think she didn't know that?

I can't stay here.

She slid the seaweed mush onto a linen cloth.

Eventually the locals will work out who I am.

She folded up the seaweed with herbs, some dried mushroom, and tied it up in a little pouch.

We could disguise ourselves. We can cross to Scotland. Then go on south.

Dropped it in the beer.

If I took some things from the monastery, some money, some silver to sell.

Constantinople is a long way, she said.

The mead would steep now for a few weeks.

There's always work for a soldier there. Besides—

Besides what?

I have this.

He took the reliquary from under his tunic. He'd polished the box. The clean silver caught even this dull interior light. It glistened.

I could sell it. Buy a boat. Become a jarl.

She looked at him.

What do you think?

His eyes were down, his voice casual.

Does it matter what I think?

Of course.

She hated seeing him make himself stupid like this.

You're a man. You do what you want to do. You don't need my permission.

She bustled past him out into the misty rain and back to the cottage.

Wait! Una! Una!

She shut the door hard behind her.

That didn't go well, he reflected.

Still, this mead smelled good even in its raw state. He dipped a ladle in the jar. An oakwood in autumn slid down his throat. Then a barn owl crying in the night. Finally, the slight aftertaste of fear.

He drank some more.

★

She woke up and the bed was empty. He sat by the hearth poking at embers with a stick. She watched him in the firelight.

What's wrong?

He'll come back.

Who?

Helgi.

Not tonight, though.

She got up, carrying the blanket, and went to sit beside him.

Not tonight. But he'll come, and all this will have to end.

His hair was badly cut. His shirt, stretched across his back, was grubby and torn. His feet were bare. He was a peasant, not a pirate.

She sat close, pulled the blanket over them, threw a peat on the fire.

Spark and crackle.

How did he get his name?

Helgi?

Cleanshirt?

What do you mean?

His nickname — does he not like blood on his shirt? Or does he clean the blood of his victims with his shirt? Or does he kill nobles whose shirts are clean? Or is it worse than that?

Worse?

Does he make women clean the blood of their husbands off his clothes?

No.

What then?

There was already a guy called Helgi on his uncle's boat. One trip, that guy spilt stew on himself. So, he was Helgi Dirtyshirt. When Helgi Gustafsson joined up, we needed a name to distinguish him, so we called him Helgi Cleanshirt.

That's all?

You have some very strange ideas about Vikings.

I know, but . . .

We're not all about murder, you know.

She leaned into his stupid body. *Will you go to Constantinople?*

No.

Come to bed.

He came to bed.

Chapter 19

It wasn't many days after that, as they sat on a wooden bench in the church eating bread and broth, when Martin remarked to Grimur that God was all around them.

Grimur said he would expect as much since this was literally God's house and so one would expect it to be where He lived.

Martin said, no, that wasn't what he meant. God was in the church, but He was also everywhere. He was on the land, in the woods, on the beaches, on the sea.

Everywhere on *I*.

Grimur remarked that, presumably, that's what Saint Columba had noticed. That *I* was the sort of place God would like. The way a man has a house but can also like a farm or a hunting ground and so, obviously, God would want to spend time on *I* and we could expect to find Him here.

Martin said, no, that still wasn't what he meant. Martin said he meant that God was all around us, present, wholly and completely, in every single corner of the whole world at all times.

Even in the middle of the sea?

Even in the middle of the sea.

God loves us, said Martin. *God is love. He is what we are. He is what we are not. He's in you and He's outside us. He's all things that are the world, and He's all things that are not the world. God is beyond our understanding, and yet inside every one of us is a divine ember, a holy flame, waiting to be reunited with Him in the divine light of the Messiah.*

Grimur thought about this.

Martin continued. *There is no limit to God. He is eternal, endless, unfathomable.*

Endless?

Martin nodded. *Endless.*

Grimur was silent for a moment. Then he put down his soup bowl. *I don't like it*, he said, *I don't want to know this. Don't tell me any more.*

He left the church, his bread unfinished.

Martin ate the bread.

After a moment, Grimur stormed back in. His eyes were full of fire. He was a warrior again.

The world is not love. The world is the opposite of love.

Grimur held the boy. *Have you ever seen an eagle take a lamb?*

The boy shook his head.

They tear open the belly and eat the lamb alive from the inside. Then crows eat the eyes. Foxes take the rest. All the while the ewe stands by the corpse, sick with untaken milk, bleating. Is that love?

The world is indifferent to us. The world is lust and fists and teeth and rock and tide and plague. Everything wants to kill you. Everything that happens to us is woven in a tapestry by three immortal women who hang it on the wall of a hall full of gods who barely, if ever, look at it. The world is not love. The world is a tree, heavy with fruit, with a bear at the bottom and an eagle at the top.

Grimur let the boy go.

Helgi is coming!

Martin stared at him wide-eyed. No longer a priest — a frightened child, suddenly, who barely had the balls to grow a moustache.

Helgi is coming and I have forgotten my gods!

*

That night Grimur went to the stable and bridled Lady Grey, the old white mare. Midges clouded round him. He ignored them. Her hooves echoed on the flagstones as they crossed the courtyard. Enjoying the light of the full moon, she let out a low whinny. He shushed her and patted her neck and walked her into the church.

Una woke. She'd heard a loud horse-shout in the yard. Had one got out? She moved her hand in the dark to find Grimur. He wasn't there. He must be dealing with it. He was a good man.

She turned to the wall and fell back to sleep.

*

The sky lightened a little.

Martin rose for Lauds.

He pulled a cloak over his shoulder. The season had turned. Clouds hurried overhead.

And then he smelt blood.

JESUS!

The white mare hung from the cross of Saint John. Her neck cut open. Her head splayed back. The foot of the cross was puddled with blood, stinking and fly-ridden. Red handprints were smeared all over the stone.

The remains of a peat fire smouldered nearby. Burnt meat and grease spattered the blackened stones. A trail of gore led to the church door.

Martin went inside. As his eyes adjusted to the light, he saw. In front of the altar, his body covered in dried blood, Grimur knelt naked. He was singing in his own language an odd deep rumbling song that seemed to come through him rather than from him.

Martin stared at him, utterly bewildered. *Brother Grimur?*

Grimur opened his eyes. He saw the pale boy shake in fear. He spoke simply. *I have some obligations to observe. I'm sorry. It will be over soon.*

Grimur closed his eyes and resumed his song.

Martin stumbled, horrified, back out into the yard.

★

Una found the Viking naked and snoring on the stone floor. He stank of blood and mead and meat. She was angry because she had liked the mare. Lady Grey still had some years of life left in her. It had been cruel to kill her, and a waste.

But Grimur was in another world. He wouldn't be back for a while.

She covered him in blankets and laid a bowl by his head.

For the rest of the day, she cleaned the church and sluiced the yard.

Chapter 20

When October comes, whales swim through the Sound of
I, chasing sprats. Their bodies are dark against the light blue
sand-lit water. The wind and the waves hide their long sad
calls.

The only thing that gives away their presence is a trail of
cloud puffs over the water

dot dot dot

*

Martin stayed away from Grimur.

The horse death had changed the boy. Bleak now, he
saw no love in God, only justice. He was consumed now
with one purpose. He must finish *John the Apostle* before the
Northmen came back and he was martyred for God.

Time passed unkept. The bell hung unstruck. The offices
of the day went by unsung. There was no other task.

Martin sat in the scriptorium and wrote.

He copied each word a dozen times on wood before
he carefully placed it onto the parchment. In this way he
completed the final verses and chapters of the scripture.

As he wrote, he repeated the verses he was working on, over and over, in his head.

Una brought meals. Martin barely ate.

The edge between this world and the world of the Lord seemed to him to have become almost transparent.

The Holy Spirit worked next to him, in him, through him, filled him. It was a presence so utterly beautiful and compassionate and courageous and good that sometimes Martin would weep, and his tears would blot the letters on which he was working and he would have to begin the whole page again.

But he didn't mind.

He was becoming one with the eternal.

He was not-becoming not-one with the not-eternal.

A number of days, possibly weeks, passed during which he lost all boundaries of himself. Before, on the seventeenth of November 826 Anno Domini, he finished the last letter of the last word of the last sentence of the *Holy Gospel of John the Apostle*.

I was complete.

And Martin was – finally and completely – whole.

Chapter 21

Autumn came on a Tuesday.

The air was colder that morning, some leaves had fallen in the grove, and the night's wind had flattened the bracken.

Lines of geese crossed the sky in straggled runes.

★

Una went out looking for ingredients. Nothing in particular, but autumn was a good time for gathering. Bluster pulled at her hair as she bashed through the heather and bog over to Saint Colm's Bay. The world that morning was an excited child, alive and demanding her attention. She felt full and whole and capable and wise.

She smiled.

Not that she noticed. If she'd noticed, she would almost certainly have stopped. Smiling had not been part of Una's life since the smith first hit her. To smile was to invite a blow, or sarcasm, or just some later cruelty. The smith was an unhappy soul, and he couldn't bear to see in others the joy he denied himself. So, if he heard her hum as she worked, or giggle, or take pleasure in a colour or a texture, he would invariably destroy the thing that caused it.

It was the same with the children. He cowed them, hammered them and bent their spirits all out of shape. Although she had found ways to love them, tiny acts he couldn't spot, he was a craftsman of lies as well as iron and he had told them their mother was wicked, stupid and not to be trusted, and so, as they grew, they withdrew from her completely. When they finally left for the mainland and marriage, it was a relief. It's easier to love an absent child than a child who's present but cold.

So, Una was not used to feeling pleasure without it being accompanied by dread. Yet here she was, alive on *I*, on an autumn morning, replete, content, at one with the world.

Whole.

Reaching higher ground, she sat on a rock amongst the heather and watched the laverocks rising and falling, singing to each other in the gusts.

And then she noticed a flash of red on the sea.

Red? That was odd.

There it was again. A flash of red.

It was a sail.

On heavy swell.

A red sail.

*

Grimur was milking.

Blossom, Honey, Sorrel, Heather and Daisy milled

around, talking cheerfully to him in cow. *Moo. Maa. Oom. Ehh. Moo.*

Grimur liked autumn. Soon it would be time to take the beasts indoors. Cosy.

He noticed Una had come back early.

It's getting colder. Tomorrow I'll start making the cottage ready for winter.

Don't.

Why not?

He tried to read her smileless face.

I saw a red sail.

Grimur sank down onto the straw.

★

The Lord will look after us.

The Lord has no war band! moaned Grimur.

The Good Lord needs no war band, pagan, for He has the service of our heart and faith.

Martin was still angry with Grimur for desecrating the church. He was also intoxicated with pride that he had, at long last, completed his book.

Frankly, I'm happy Helgi is coming. It's an honour I've been waiting for, the coming of the hour when my own poor worthless blood might water holy I in the name of Jesus Christ.

His cassock seemed to puff with his insufferable pomposity as he strode into church for Prime.

This is Helgi we're talking about, you fucking moron. Helgi Cleanshirt. He invents ways to kill people the way fine craftsmen work gold. The last time he was here, you were so afraid you hid in a shit pit. I'm telling you: take your chance to run.

I will not abandon Saint Colm.

Martin stood before the altar and began to belt out a hymn for Prime:

Bow down Your ear, O Lord, and hear me!
For I am poor and I am needy!
Preserve my soul; for I am holy!

Odin's bones! Grimur grabbed him. *Saint Colm is gone, Godfish.*

Saint Colm is all around us, Viking.

No, he's not!

He is!

I found the casket.

What?

I found his reliquary on Dùn Ì. There is no finger in it. The box is empty.

Martin held his speech as steady as he could. *You opened the box?*

It's all crumbled to dust. The flesh long gone. Nothing living lasts — you know that, Martin.

You should never have opened the box.

But I did.

Martin turned his back on Grimur.

Brother Martin. Brother Martin. Friend Martin. Martin . . .

But he would not turn.

In the days of my trouble, I will call upon You,
for I know You will answer me.
Among the gods there's none like You, O Lord,
And no creation more wondrous than Yours.

Grimur left him to his useless tunes and fought the gusts across the yard back to Una.

The cottage was warm. Una had prepared food for them. What else could she do?

We could leave, he offered.

My bees are here.

We could hide.

They'd find us.

We could fight.

They'd overwhelm us.

If only they could shut the door and pretend to be dead. If only they could stop time, interrupt the weaving women, just for a moment, change the thread.

Grimur threw a stone into the fire.

It bounced and hit the cauldron, which gave out a fearful *ding*.

What, then?

We welcome them.

Una outlined to him her plan.

★

She came back from the stores with some flour in a bowl.

Grimur stood naked by the fire.

She took a soft handful and patted it into his chest. A

cloud of powder haloed his face. She patted some onto his stomach, then his back, his thighs, his feet, his face. Handful after handful of flour, she smeared and rubbed and threw over his body, till the air was filled with white dust like they were in Heaven.

When she was finished, he was pale as Lady Grey.

Now put on your war gear, tie up the boy and wait for me in the church.

Grimur hit his chest. *Ho!*

White dust clouded and danced.

Chapter 22

The red-sailed wave horse galloped over the silver girdle of the islands, sending spray and wild snorts in its wake.

Helgi stood on the prow and looked *I*-ward.

He liked attacking monks. He felt a swell of energy as he led his men towards a monastery, a surging confluence of the three great rivers of his soul: gold, gods and going on raids.

A Viking had to raid. That was the job, really. One didn't necessarily have to love the work. But Helgi did. Whenever he torched some village or other, Helgi felt at one with nature: he was wind, wave, war. The people Helgi attacked resisted of course; they fought, they struggled, they cried out to their gods. The bird eats the mouse. The fox eats the bird. Each of us plays our role in the mighty dance of life.

Helgi thought of his victims the way a hunter thinks of birds. He liked them; they made nice noises. He would always offer prayers and a sacrifice of slaves in honour of those he'd raided when his men returned to Shetland.

Helgi didn't fear death. In the sword storm, he was neither in this world nor the other. He was alive in both and dead in neither. What was life anyway, if it wasn't a dream, dreamt by someone somewhere on the other side? A shifting of dancers from one side of a hall to the other?

Monks, though, were different. Helgi despised monks. Monks were vermin, living like parasites off the labour of others. Monks didn't protect their villages. Monks didn't raid or farm or fish or fix.

Every village has a beggar, someone whose body or mind is so broken that they're incapable of work. Normally, such unfortunates are looked after, found tasks for which they're capable. They might become night soil removers or bards. Something useful. But these monks were quite capable of normal work. They were sons of noble men. They had access to weapons and women and land. Yet, despite all these gifts, they'd turned their backs on the dance of life and climbed up their own behinds. They lived in thought. They offered nothing to anybody. They sang for their own pleasure. Their poetry went unshared. They kept their cocks for themselves. They offered a description of the world which simply did not match reality.

Love? Give me strength.

Christianity was like berserker piss. You drank it, you felt special, then you woke up three days later naked in a forest with no memory at all of how you got there.

No, monks were different. Monks were rich self-indulgers who chose a life of tiresome solipsistic whimsy. As far as Helgi was concerned, monks represented everything that was wrong with the world today.

★

A great shout broke over the pale sand . . .

Ho!

. . . and the sword stainers and raven feeders of Helgi's mob laid down their long sea feet and jumped from the fore-deck to the shore.

Buttercock, Bloodnose, Eyeballs, Gore Dog, Puffin Face, One Ear, Chin Slitter, Fuck-a-Whale, Lead Fist, Fat Dog, Denmark, Horse Boy, Lady Legs, Thumb Cracker and Brown Pants – the men of Helgi Cleanshirt's boat – breathed in, filled their bones with life-lust, heaved and shouted together:

Ho!

Ho! Ho! Ho!

Shorty had died in June after a demon sent a cleg to fill his body with pus; Madhead drowned showing off in Shetland; and no one knew what had happened to Ghost Axe, but one day he just wasn't there any more.

Let's do this quickly! Helgi said.

Two shares of silver to whoever guts the first Godfish! Denmark yelled.

Kill the fuckers! the men roared back, and the gang of Nordic nightmare-providers jogged gently along the coast to the church.

*

It was much colder today than the last time they raided.

There was a light dusting of frost on the high parts of Dùn Ì. Buttercock's hands were numb without gloves, Bloodnose felt his stiff knee playing up and Horse Boy's teeth were chattering.

Helgi ran in the lead.

What a sight he was! His war helmet shining, his big sword held high, his leather gauntlets polished and stiff, his long hair combed beautifully, his beard sparkling with frost and fine jewellery.

Was any warrior ever more blessed by the gods than Helgi Gustafsson? Was any island more in need of submission than *Ì*? Was any raid more blessed than this?

No, thought Helgi Cleanshirt. This is going to be a terrific day!

And that was when he saw the ghost.

Chapter 23

Helgi stopped stock-still and stuck his sword out in front of him, his hands shaking.

The other men formed a semi-circle around him and stared in horror at the phantom in front of them who held out his pale hand and called them to halt.

Lads! Lads! Good to see you! The apparition leered at them horribly.

Helgi replied as if addressing a jarl. *Who speaks to us, sir?*
It's me.

The warriors murmured among themselves for a moment.

Gunnar? offered Puffin Face. *Is it Gunnar?*

No, it's me . . . Grimur.

Grimur? Helgi looked at Denmark. Denmark was usually good with names.

The old raider searched his memory. *Grimur Eriksson?*
No!

Denmark shrugged. They all looked at each other, bewildered. Until it dawned on Buttercock.

No-Name!

Yes! Yes!

Grimur and Buttercock did a little bee-wiggle dance for each other, a little ritual of recognition.

Lads, it's our old comrade, Grimur No-Name! Don't you remember? We buried him on the raid in spring.

In truth the lads didn't remember, but clearly it was true. Besides, no one wants to argue with the undead, so everybody cheered and welcomed him back to the world.

Ho, Grimur! Ho, Grimur! Ho, Grimur!

Buttercock went to embrace his old shipmate, but Grimur stepped back.

Comrades, don't touch me! I'm dead. If you touch me, you'll be pulled in to join me on the other side.

Helgi's hands were still shaking. *So, what happened to you, No-Name, my old friend? Why are you not in Odin's hall, enjoying your feasting and fighting and fucking with the heroes?*

Long story short – magic mead. It allows me to travel. I live half the year with Odin in Valhalla, where I do all the usual things as you describe. Then half the year I come here, where I have a woman and a slave and an endless supply of magic mead. Why don't I tell you all about it over dinner?

Dinner? Gore Dog was confused.

Do ghosts eat? Brown Pants asked.

Ha ha! I see. No, of course not. All my sustenance comes from the gods. But my woman and her slave are mortal, and so are you, and you have come a long way, and you need to eat so come, come

and taste my hospitality. Last night we slaughtered a cow. Come to
my hall. We'll eat, drink, sing!

The men looked to Helgi.

Helgi sheathed his sword.

Chapter 24

The church was full of smoke, sweat, beer stink and men. Vikings sat on upturned pews and ate from wooden plates. Softened with drink, satiated with meat and barley, they burped, flopped, wept, laughed and pissed in the corners.

To Odin! shouted Grimur.

To Odin! they shouted back.

To Helgi Cleanshirt! shouted Grimur.

To Helgi Cleanshirt! they shouted back.

Moving amongst them, almost invisibly, Una poured ladleful after ladleful of her best mead into the Viking drinking horns.

Martin watched from the nave.

He was tied up like a pig for slaughter. It was stupid of him ever to have trusted a Viking. God must have wanted to punish him for his pride. Now, finally, he faced his martyrdom. He was hoping they might cut his throat, but, with these monsters, anything was possible.

He felt lucky that they hadn't, at least so far, roasted him on a spit and eaten him.

It was strange to see the church so full of light and life but in such a horrible inversion of its holy purpose. A dozen male voices sang, but in Norse not in Irish. They cursed rather than prayed. Mead and meat was their sacrament. Debauchery, not love, was their purpose.

The pews creaked with the weight of warriors and their leather armour. The floor screamed with metal weapons scraped along the flagstones. The holy sanctuary, now full, foul and corrupt, was, Martin shuddered, the very image of sin.

Suddenly there was a shout.

Lads! Lads!

Grimur rose and stood on the altar, his boots sullying the sacred marble. In his arms he held a silver box.

There was a moment of silence, and for a second you might think it was a church again.

Sixteen Sons of Thor! Sixteen Suppliers of Sleeplessness! Traders of Tears! Sword Forest of Shetland! Sixteen Tree-Beams Who Hold Up the Moon! Sixteen Links in Earth's Silver Necklace! Lads! You've travelled the whale trail and climbed sea mountains. You've passed under the Eagle Castles of Hoy, and through the Burst Green Bones of Ness. You deserve your cargo of praise, not dung from a dying old eagle. You deserve the best whisky from the cups of the undead, and you deserve treasure. So, to reward you for your loyalty to the old gods, and to thank you for your visit, I, Grimur No-Name, lately of Valhalla, am proud to offer you . . . Columba's bones!

Grimur raised up the reliquary to shine in the firelight. The Northmen banged their axe shafts on the floor. Martin felt sick.

Stepping down from the broken altar, Grimur presented Helgi with the reliquary.

Awestruck, Helgi examined the silver box. He stroked the burnished metal. He fingered the complex metalwork of its making. He saw his own red face, illuminated briefly in its warm reflection. Then he put it down beside him on the floor.

Grimur, you have the favour of the fates. You have the favour of the fates. Whatever your dealings in the other world, you've brought us silver, and we are indebted. We'll keep a seat for you in the front rank now.

Helgi raised his drinking horn. *To Grimur No-Name!* he shouted.

To Grimur No-Name! the men shouted back.

And they banged down their axe shafts again and again and again and again.

★

Grimur grabbed Martin by the hood of his cowl and shook him. *Look at this little bastard Godfish. I made him my slave!*

Do you fuck him? shouted Lady Legs.

Sometimes. Why not?

The men roared with laughter.

Una moved among them, pouring more and more mead.

Can we fuck him, too? shouted Chin Slitter, more for comic effect than from desire, although he was curious.

Later, dear friend. Later, you can slide in between those Christian flesh hills. But before that, I want to show off my Christ slave in another way, because he has a gift, a gift for song.

The men fell quiet.

Grimur pulled Martin's face close to his and hissed to him in Irish: *Sing!*

What? Martin was confused.

Anything. Just do it. Do it for Jesus. Do it for God.

Martin looked at the room of men. His heart juddered. He felt his legs drain of strength.

He realised Grimur had untied his bonds.

*

It was, he supposed, the hour of Matins. He rose. He stood before his perverted congregation.

> *Lord, if you open my lips, my mouth shall declare Your*
> *   praise.*
> *My soul faints for Your salvation,*
> *but I hope in Your word.*
> *My eyes fail for Your word, saying,*
> *When will You comfort me?*
> *For I am become like a bottle in the smoke,*
> *yet do I not forget You.*
> *How many days have I left as Your servant?*
> *When will You punish those who persecute me?*
> *Blessed is our Lord Jesus Christ. Amen.*
> *Alleluia, alleluia.*
> *Alleluia, alleluia.*
> *Alleluia, alleluia.*

Martin's plainsong rose and fell. The melody wound its way round the room like a rope. They felt the otherworld in it. Without noticing, they all relaxed and, slowly, one by one, they fell asleep.

*

Viking bodies lay all around the church.

It would have looked like the scene of a bloody massacre had it not been accompanied by the pig snuffles, snorts, raspberries and flesh drones of the slumbering drunkards.

Martin gawped at the scene. *It's a miracle.*

It's not a miracle, said Una. *It's mead. I used to make it for the smith. If he was angry or afraid, or if I needed quiet, I'd give it to him. He'd sleep. The dreams are sweet. When he woke, he would be confused and docile.*

Martin looked at her with suspicion. *I cannot be involved with witchcraft.*

Not witchcraft, said Una. *Craft.*

Martin was unclear where the difference lay.

They'll be knocked out for a couple of hours, at least.

Together they laid out the sleeping men in straight lines along the floor.

*

When they were finished, Grimur drew a sword from Fuck-a-Whale's hip.

Farewell, friend.

He pointed the tip at the sleeping man's neck and prepared to push.

No! Martin interrupted. *There will be no killing.*

Even Martin was surprised at the certainty of his command. It was almost, he thought, as if Jesus had spoken, using him as His voice.

Grimur was testy. *We don't have time to be Christian, Brother Martin. These are sixteen of the best warriors in the world. If we don't send them to Odin now, they'll wake and kill us all in minutes.*

It's a sin for a monk to shed blood.

I'm not a monk.

It's a sin to kill in a church.

I can take them outside.

Christ calls for mercy.

Grimur didn't know how to respond to this odd catechism. He liked Martin very much. He was drawn to the boy's god. But Viking work is not the business of Godfish. This was a problem for men who feed ravens.

Odin calls for blood.

Grimur felt he had won the argument. He looked at the boy, expecting to see humility. He also felt that Una's planning, and his excellent execution, had resulted in an unlikely victory for the Church. The sort of victory one might expect to be sung about in Christian halls for some time. Not criticised over nit-picky points of theology.

Bind them. This was Una. *There's plenty more rope in the stables.*

Now it was two against one.

Grimur considered. *Whatever you say.*

Una and Martin gathered the men's weapons.

★

Grimur returned to the church, ropes dangling from him like giant squid tentacles. It took a moment for his eyes to adjust to the dark. The hall was damp and warm and smelled of mead sweat, sleep fart, charred meat and the sea. Grimur had forgotten how much he liked that smell.

He smiled.

He saw the altar caught in soft grey light and he saw Una.

Why was she tied up? Why was her mouth bound? Why were her eyes lit with fear?

At that moment he caught the faint scent of a stale perfume. He recognised it but couldn't place it. Like hearing a familiar old song far, far away.

Grimur instinctively turned and saw Helgi. His axe raised high, running at him, roaring full berserker.

This wasn't good.

Chapter 25

Every Viking has a Valkyrie. These are the women war spirits who shadow men in battle. Your Valkyrie decides whether you live or die and, if you are to die, they decide how.

Grimur's Valkyrie was Old Tit Scratcher.

She was one of the less glamorous of the shield maidens, well into her later years, with a scent like vinegar wine, but she was good at her job. You could have a younger Valkyrie if you like, but this one was experienced, devious, filled with fury, and she really, really, really didn't like losing.

As soon as Grimur entered the church, Old Tit Scratcher had sensed something was wrong and roused him from his dwam. Just in time, he ducked Helgi's charge.

The axe stuck in the door, and Helgi's own force drove him into the door after it.

Grimur was stunned. What had gone wrong? Now they were all going to die.

No one fought Helgi Cleanshirt and survived.

Helgi freed his axe and turned to face Grimur, who stepped back, tripped over the sleeping Gore Dog and fell arse backwards onto the flagstones.

Una groaned. She liked Grimur. This was going to be hard.

Helgi loomed over him.

Are you going to kill me?

I thought you were already dead?

Yes, that's right, no point, Grimur offered hopefully.

Instead, I'm going to chop up your corpse and feed you to pigs.

Helgi raised the axe above his head.

Dagger! hissed Old Tit Scratcher.

Grimur grabbed his dagger from inside his britches and rolled to the right, just as Helgi's axe crashed hard onto his left arm, cutting his hand off at the wrist.

Bollocks, muttered Old Tit Scratcher.

Una winced. A hand was a bad limb to lose in a fight. Another blow, and Grimur would be finished. She willed Martin to come back. He'd gone to the beach to shout across the sound in the hope of summoning help. Although, if Martin did come back, she was unclear what he might be able to achieve. Maybe a miracle?

Grimur screamed. His body was flooded with white light. He stared at his hand lying on the floor beside him, useless.

Old Tit Scratcher kicked him back to his senses.

In one quick, instinctive movement, Grimur closed his eyes and thrust his dagger vaguely upwards as hard as he could. It was Helgi's bad fortune that, in the very same moment, he had decided to stand astride Grimur, legs triumphantly apart, bracing himself for a simple death strike to the prone man's head. This moment of over-confidence meant Grimur's wild stab ended up connecting with Helgi's crotch, severing the tendons at the top of his thigh and puncturing his ball sack.

Helgi dropped to the floor and curled up into himself like a rose in the night.

Did he whimper? He might have whimpered.

This sort of thing was inevitable, thought Una. Men could be strong, they could be clever, but when there's sharp metal flying around, someone's bound to get their ball sack punctured in the end, and it's just an accident of the dance whether it's you or the other guy.

Thank God, this time it was the other guy.

Grimur struggled to his feet and made his way over to Una. What the hell is he doing now? she thought, as he wobbled towards her, blood spurting from his butchered wrist stump.

He dropped to his knees and cut her wrist bonds.

As he did it, he looked into her eyes.

Such nice eyes, she thought.

As soon as her hands were free, she whipped off the cloth gag and moved to kiss him.

Old Tit Scratcher slapped them both back to reality.

He's not dead!

What?

Una pointed to the church doorway.

Helgi had risen from his pain pool and was standing now, leaning heavily on his axe. He began limping to the door in an attempt to escape.

Chapter 26

The October night was bright and crisp and cold. The yard, a pool of silver moonlight. An owl screeched from the stable roof.

Helgi staggered across the yard, every step a spear of fierce pain in his groin. He considered his situation. No-Name had been lucky, but he was a weak and cowardly fighter. If Helgi could find shelter, just for a moment, bind his wound, drink some spirits and gather his senses, he would be able to recover sufficiently to kill him properly, then the boy monk and finally the woman.

He paused to rest on the stone cross of Saint John, hot blood pooling in his boots. He had never been in as much pain as he was now. The rough stone of the cross felt as cool and comforting to him as skin. He wanted nothing more than to slide down and sleep on its welcoming base. Maybe he would even become Christian. His joke amused him. He laughed, and his groin exploded. His mind filled with stars and fire.

Odin, what's happening!

He put his hand into his britches and felt a warm mess of blood and meat. A lump of wet flesh came loose in his palm. Resting his head on the cross, he lifted out his hand to see what it was and, opening his palm, he saw, lying in a bright red puddle of blood, his soft grey cock.

Fuck.

He'd held his cock often but never this close to his face.

Cleanshirt! Cleanshirt! Cleanshirt!

Grimur emerged from the church. His bloody stump was bound tight with Una's headscarf. In his right hand he held a heavy axe. He heaved himself across the yard.

Helgi put his soft cock in his jacket pocket, braced himself with his back against the cross and brought his axe into a two-handed grip.

Grimur lumbered right at him, the fat old bull.

Helgi swung at just the right moment to catch Grimur on the hip. It wasn't a strong enough blow to cut through his big leather belt, but it brutally broke bones, and Grimur flew sideways, landing face down in mud.

Grimur's stumpy left arm now lay near Helgi's boot, so he stamped on it hard. It made a satisfying crunch, and Grimur yelped like a beaten dog.

Unfortunately, for Helgi, the effort unbalanced him, and his wounded right leg gave way. He now fell in the mud as well. He dragged himself across the yard like a three-legged fox looking for a place of safety.

Grimur felt as though his bowels had given way and his

insides were falling out. He pulled himself through the mud and gave chase.

In fairness, neither man was moving very fast.

Each yard of ground was won with massive expenditure of life force. Each aimed thudding, wild axe blows at the other, none of which made target but each of which bled yet more precious energy from their weakening bodies.

Each man heard his Valkyrie in his ear sing, *One of you dies tonight, tonight. One of you dies tonight . . .*

After about fifteen minutes of this, Helgi made it to the scriptorium, pulled himself inside and barred the door.

★

Slowly, painfully, Grimur tried to crack the door with his axe. It would not give. Helgi had jammed a chair behind it.

Fuck you, No-Name! Helgi yelled from inside.

Fuck you, No-Balls! Grimur countered – wittily, he thought – but he was cursing under his breath as he tried to work out a way into the building. His stump was starting to hurt badly now. He was feeling very faint.

His thoughts were broken by a roar.

Watch the roof, Viking!

Old Tit Scratcher had seen it just in time. Helgi had set the scriptorium on fire. A ball of burning thatch fell to the ground beside him. Flame had taken so quickly it drew the air upwards in a fierce bellows wind and it threw sparks up into the night a dozen yards high.

The book, thought Grimur, the book!

*

Thump! Thump! Thump!

Grimur shoulder-barged the door, over and over and over. Each strike sent a lightning bolt down his arm. Every breath drew in a lungful of hot, stinking smoke. Sweat and ash merged on his forehead and flowed into his eyes.

Brother Grimur, come away from the fire!

Martin had run back from the beach when he saw the flames. Finding Una, they'd both filled pails at the cattle troughs, and each now desperately threw water on the flames.

They might as well have wept to quench the fires of Hell.

Grimur, come away! Una cried out.

The book's in there! he yelled back.

Forget the book! Martin shouted.

Even Old Tit Scratcher gave up on him now. War, she enjoyed. Suicide, not so much.

But Grimur would not forget the book.

Grimur was a Viking. *Thump*. Grimur was a pagan. *Thump*. Grimur was an old man. *Thump*. Grimur had no arm. *Thump*. Grimur had no name. *Thump*. But Grimur still had the majority of a fat old body and the entirety of a stupid heart, and he would not let the word of God burn because of Helgi fucking Cleanshirt.

Thump!

The door frame cracked and caved inwards, with Grimur propelled after it into the furnace.

Fire was pouring down the walls from the roof. Smoke swirled everywhere. Grimur saw the book on the writing table. It was covered with cloth, as it was every night. Miraculously, no sparks had yet fallen on it.

He staggered into the depths of the flames, his skin crackling in the heat. He laid his good hand on the book and clutched its weight to his chest. Then he turned to get out.

Helgi blocked the door.

Framed by flame, his skin purple, Helgi smelt of cooked pork. His beard and hair glowed from caught sparks. His mouth was a skull's grin of pain, but his eyes were alive with pleasure.

He brandished a long fighting dagger.

Come on, No-Name, let us enter Valhalla together.

This was annoying.

Grimur didn't want to go to Valhalla. He wanted to go to Una. He wanted to spend eternity in a cow-warmed cottage drinking mead and laughing at jokes. Now he was going to die because this half-roasted Viking imbecile just didn't know when to stop.

Helgi roared, and a bit of his face fell off.

Grimur charged at him with all the strength he had left.

Helgi thrust the fighting knife.

The blade hit the book.

The book hit Helgi, who was knocked backwards and fell onto burning timbers.

Grimur stumbled over the prone body as he made for

the door, jamming his heel into Helgi's burst balls as he did so. Helgi screamed in what must surely have been pain, but which, due to his berserker grin and weakened voice, came out as a gasp of sensual pleasure.

Away from the flames, Grimur flung himself out onto the cold ground. Martin and Una dragged him away.

The roof of the scriptorium collapsed, and the rest of the building fell around it.

Helgi's bliss was complete.

He was – at last – whole.

*

Ashes blew on the wind.

The screech owl crossed the yard.

I fell into darkness.

Chapter 27

Martin, Una and Grimur lay together on straw, a heap of limbs. A cow pissed in the corner. Steam rose into the morning air.

The peace was broken by a flurry of male voices. The door flew open, and daylight poured in.

Una opened her eyes, blinking and headachey.

Are you alive?

It was Domhnall of Crinan. It was, she felt, a stupid question. *Yes.*

Where is Helgi Cleanshirt?

Martin and Grimur now awoke, befuddled.

Helgi Cleanshirt is dead, said Una.

The room was filling up with men Una didn't recognise. They carried heavy weapons but these were not Northmen, nor were they from Mull. These were Irish men. They wore the cross.

Who killed him?

God, Martin replied, and his voice seemed, to Domhnall, to have gained in authority since he last heard him speak.

At any rate, his answer seemed to satisfy the king's man, closing, as it did, any need for further investigation.

From outside a woman's voice called: *Domhnall! Domhnall!*

Martin recognised it.

Domhnall, come see! There's a dozen Northmen bound captive on the church floor!

The voice's possessor pushed into the room and the armed men gave way for her.

A woman with red hair.

Brother Martin?

Sister Bronagh?

I thought you must be dead.

So did I.

★

The men in the room were Bronagh's brothers, warriors of the Dál Fiatach.

Now that she no longer harboured dreams of being an anchoress, she had, on her return to Ireland, persuaded her uncle, the king, that he should found a new monastery near Armagh. She also suggested that he should equip it with a nunnery of which she would be Mother Abbess. As for the monastery, she had a good idea as to who should come to be Father Abbott.

Her uncle had agreed to this for several reasons. One, because her theological arguments struck him as sound; two, because he took her point that it would give him glory amongst kings; and three, because he knew she would never stop going on about it if he didn't.

So, now she had returned across the sea with her brothers as escort, only to find the island once again a smoking ruin.

The book?

It's here. Martin fetched from under the straw the wrapped package.

Bronagh took it from him. Opened it and turned the first page. *It's beautiful.*

Who made this? asked Domhnall.

God, said Martin.

Chapter 28

Bronagh's brothers led a chain of bound Vikings down to the boats.

Buttercock, Bloodnose, Eyeballs, Gore Dog, Puffin Face, One Ear, Chin Slitter, Fuck-a-Whale, Lead Fist, Fat Dog, Denmark, Horse Boy, Lady Legs, Thumb Cracker and Brown Pants would be taken to Armagh and sold. Stripped of their coloured clothes, their beard decorations, their shields and their swords, these trees of the spear looked like what they were . . .

Men.

Grimur couldn't meet their gaze. *I should have killed them.*

You showed mercy, said Martin.

But Martin was wrong. Slaves couldn't enter Valhalla when they died. Instead, they went to a hall of their own. A hall which was fine and comfortable, but which held no glory. Grimur knew this because Fat Eye had told him after he killed his father. By not killing the Vikings last night, he had condemned them instead to an eternity of shame.

There was no point explaining this to Martin.

★

Sickly smoke still hung in the air.

Domhnall sat beside Una on the low wall. *The bishop in Kilmartin has heard about you. He's tasted your work. His own mead wife is old. He wants your brew. If you come to Kilmartin, he'll look after you well.*

I don't make the brew — the bees make it.

There are bees at Kilmartin.

You have bees, but you don't have this . . . She gestured across the island that lay before them. Meadow, machair, heather, seaweed, rock, oak, rowan . . . I *makes the brew. The brew is* I.

★

Bronagh found Martin among the oaks, kneeling by the grave mound of Father Abbot Blathmac.

Quietly, she sat nearby.

The wind had dropped. Autumn sun illuminated the grove and dappled it. She studied him as he rocked and mumbled a melancholic litany under his breath. He was a soft boy, but so serious. The men in her life were the opposite. His fingers were ink-stained and breakable, like learning itself. She wanted to protect it, protect him. He was a sapling now, but she could see that he could grow into a wide, tall, strong tree under which dozens might sit. But not without care. And not in this soil.

Why are you sad? she asked him.

I wanted to give my life to the Lord.

You did.

I'm still here.

You offered yourself. The Lord didn't take you.

Maybe I didn't try hard enough.

Brother Martin, you lived alone on an unprotected island for six months, while pagan pirates prowled the sea around you. If the Lord had wanted your blood, He could have taken it at any moment.

He looked at her carefully.

It was some time since he had seen the whole of her. Now he took in her whole face, her awkward coltish body, her candle-flicker soul.

There are two types of martyrdom, Brother Martin. The red martyrdom, when one gives one's life in blood, and the white martyrdom, when one gives one's life in duty. Red martyrdom is glorious, but it requires only a few moments of true faith. White martyrdom, on the other hand, requires faith for years. White martyrdom tests your strength, heart, will and soul to the limit. It is truly the gift of a life to the Lord. And, if you choose it, I am told, there will be moments of such deep rich union with Jesus as would make the stab of a sword in the gut feel as insignificant as the touch of a feather on skin.

She moved closer.

Brother Martin, the Lord loves you and trusts you and so has called you to white martyrdom. Not red.

Perhaps she was an angel, he thought.

Follow me to Armagh. God spoke to me. We will found a new house there.

This woman. He could never read her meaning. Normally he was on edge with her because her eyes were full of mischief. But now, on his knees, in the dancing light of the oak grove, he felt he knew her as well as he knew himself. He seemed to see her in all her oddness, all her curiosity.

He saw her heart for a moment, vulnerable, her expression open and clear.

Will you come? she asked.

*

As Bronagh's brothers filled the Viking boat with captives, Domhnall and his clerk took Grimur aside.

Grimur sensed it wasn't for polite small talk.

I know you're not a monk.

Grimur was about to reply, but Domhnall hushed him. *I know you're Norse. I know you were with Helgi's crew. Brother Martin told me everything.*

Oh well, thought Grimur. Just when you think the fates have woven you a life, the thread is cut. He wondered if Domhnall would behead him, enslave him or skin him alive. He very much hoped it would be option a) or b).

But before he could speak, Domhnall continued: *There are kings on the mainland who are looking for tested warriors. They would pay, and house you with the woman.*

Domhnall's clerk listened carefully as the bailiff spoke.

If you want to take your weapons and armour and leave, I'll give you a letter of passage and a new name.

Domhnall's clerk wished he were a warrior.

If you stay here, I'll number you a peasant. I will take your war axe. Your name will be Fergus McOllie.

Grimur looked at his feet.

Which is it to be?

Chapter 29

Bronagh faced Ireland – the reliquary on her knee.

She was grinning like a girl who had dipped her fingers in the pudding bowl without her mother seeing. *Shall we look inside?*

Martin sat next to her. Oar splash and wind burn flecked his face. She looked at him. His face was more mannish now. He had the beginnings of a beard. There were tiny lines at the corner of his eyes.

It's empty.

Her face fell.

The bones rotted away when the box was buried, or they were taken by a fox. I don't know. But there's nothing of the great Saint Colm left in there. It's just an empty box.

Did you look in?

No.

Then how do you know?

Grimur told me when he found it.

Bronagh hesitated. Her hair blew around her face. She opened the box.

She gasped. *Oh, Holy Mother of God.*

She turned the box around to show him.

Inside the burnished metal, on the red velvet cushion, on a tiny white linen sheet, lay a human index finger: pale, fresh, noble, slightly curled as if beckoning a soul to Heaven.

A miracle, she said.

A miracle, he replied.

⋆

Grimur found Una later, on the rocks at the top of Dùn Ì. The night was clear, and a river of stars ran in full flood around the bend of the sky. His stump had been cauterised and bound by Domhnall's clerk. He had fastened it to his breast with linen. He'd drunk a little mead.

He sat beside her.

It'll snow soon, she said.

Frost already hung in the air. The wildflowers that speckled the machair had died back. The geese had long left, leaving an eerie quiet over the machair.

The sea looks inviting.

It does.

You're a travelling man.

Not any more.

No?

It takes two hands to row. Two hands to haul a sail.

Don't you want to find your wife?

If she's alive, she thinks I'm dead.

So, what do you want to do?

I want to stay.

His heart beat heavily. He felt a throb of pain in his stump. He looked at her, this woman who had held him for a summer. This woman who made him laugh. Made him drunk.

If you'll have me.

Una gripped the cold rock. She stared out into the dark. She didn't need a man. Not a Viking, anyway. A farmer maybe, a tradesman. Grimur's only trade was war.

Will you have me?

She put her hand in his. *Right in the balls. You stabbed him right in the balls.*

I didn't mean to.

It was funny.

It was.

Right in the balls.

Yup.

Like beef on a skewer.

Don't say that.

Will he go to Valhalla?

I should think so.

Serves him right.

How?

Imagine, an eternity in a mead hall with a ripped ball sack. Every night a beautiful woman seduces you. Every night you have to say no.

Don't make me laugh. It hurts.

He leaned on her shoulder.

Their laughter lingered on the night air.

They looked towards the northern hills, looming like crimes in the memory, until eventually even those vast shapes were swallowed by the night.

Acknowledgements

In May 2022 I set off for a walk. I didn't know where I would go or what I would do except that I'd taken a month off work, had no phone, no computer and a tent on my back. It was spring, and I wanted to follow my nose.

May is normally a glorious month in Scotland. Not May 2022. It rained for three weeks without cessation. Nevertheless, I enjoyed my walk. My universe of screens fell away, and I got to know the world through feet, ears, eyes, skin. During the long damp gloaming in my tent I read, I wrote, I dreamed. I made a stick, I grew a beard.

Unsurprisingly, I ended up walking to Iona.

I would like to thank Jamie Crawford for the gift he gave me when he asked if I wanted to write a novel for this series. It was the answer to a question I hadn't known I was asking. He opened a door, and I am deeply grateful.

I thank Alison Rae for her careful and generous editing. She is a kind guide, a safety net for this writer toddling his first prose steps.

Professor Judith Jesch corresponded with me about

representations of the early medieval Norse. She introduced me to Skaldic kennings. Her book *Women in the Viking Age* is terrific, and I highly recommend it.

I would also like to acknowledge Reverend Ron Ferguson, Reverend Iain Whyte and the late Reverend Peter McDonald (not by coincidence all members of the Iona Community). Each of these patient, thoughtful men have discussed their faith with me over the years. They all made a great impression on me. They are a wonderful advert for Christianity.

My first readers were Lucie, Annie, Rory and my mum, Linda. They were encouraging, acute critics. Lucie's bee advice was invaluable. (It's important to talk to them.)

I wrote much of this book on a boat. I thank my shipmates Wendy, Mandy and Sue, three wyrd sisters who kept me company on the whale roads. I thank the elders of the round table: Jean, Jackie, Tom, Elaine, Sue, Liz, Maureen, Kathrine. I thank my wise shieldsman, Numan.

This is a Skaldic poem in praise of that boat.

Whip on my word horse, Odin,
Fill up my cup with honeyed mead
That I may praise Ambience,
That broad-haunched Ox of the deep!

No portion of glory can capture
Her smashing sea peaks
Facing the merciless cold-clad
Wolf of the willow!

Egil, lord of the seal fields,
Guides her carefully
Under the pale glow
Of heaven's cinder

He steers her bravely
Through the bones of the sea
During the black fear
Of two days joining

Drink, friends!
Take a swig of that draught
Which cheers up the ladies.
Let the mead benches groan
Under the weight of a cargo of praise.

For now we are dancing
In the great hall of the waves,
Hear the shield shakers sing,
Our tables crack, our cups spill.
Greed is dead. We have enough.

Under a thousand fires of night
I watch the silver sea road pass.
Waves of calm lap at my mind's beach,
My word hoard is empty,
My heart is full.

In Darkland Tales, the best modern Scottish authors offer dramatic retellings of stories from the nation's history, myth and legend. These are landmark moments from the past, viewed through a modern lens and alive to modern sensibilities. Each Darkland Tale is sharp, provocative and darkly comic, mining that seam of sedition and psychological drama that has always featured in the best of Scottish literature.

Rizzio Denise Mina
Hex Jenni Fagan
Nothing Left to Fear from Hell Alan Warner
Columba's Bones David Greig

DARKLAND TALES